# The Gardener of Baghdad
By Ahmad Ardalan
Copyright 2014 Ahmad Ardalan

I

*"This novel speaks about a flower...*
*The true red rose in my life,*
*The rose that represents existence, beauty and class.*
*Baghdad."*

Special thanks to Scarlett Rugers for her beautiful work on the cover.

*Two people, one city, different times; connected by a memoir. Can love exist in a city destined for decades of misery?*

Adnan leads a weary existence as a bookshop owner in modern-day, war-torn Baghdad, where bombings, corruption and assault are everyday occurrences and the struggle to survive has suffocated the joy out of life for most. But when he begins to clean out his bookshop of forty years to leave his city in search of somewhere safer, he comes across the story of Ali, the Gardener of Baghdad, Adnan rediscovers through a memoir handwritten by the gardener decades ago that beauty, love and hope can still exist, even in the darkest corners of the world.

# Table of Contents

# Chapter 1

Adnan brushed away the last shards of shattered window glass that were scattered all over the floor. It had taken six hours of effort, hard labor, to restore his bookstore to order, but finally, a new window was in place, and there was no dangerous glass shrapnel anywhere for any of his customers to step on.

Luckily for Adnan, he was in the back with a customer when the roadside bomb exploded, the third in two years. The thing exploded about 500 feet away from his store, aimed at a small gathering of workers, and it had taken its bitter toll: five casualties and dozens of injured workers in all.

*Maybe everyone is right,* Adnan considered. *Maybe it's time I close up my bookshop and leave the country like most everyone else has.* Baghdad wasn't safe anymore; it hadn't been since day the regime had changed. Not a day went by without casualties anymore, and bombs, kidnappings, and shootings were rampant. It wasn't the Iraq Adnan used to live in, the place where people could at least feel safe living with their families. The worst part about it was that the bombings and continuous conflict seemed to be for no reason, and things were just getting worse.

The questions tumbled in the disgruntled shop owner's mind: *How did this all happen? Who's behind it all? What do they stand to gain from it?* Like most Iraqis, Adnan didn't care who the ruler was or who was in charge. He'd never been into politics. He'd only wished for a nice, safe place where he and his family and their future generations could live, a place of peaceful harmony, better education, work opportunities, and free of wars.

Adnan's wife called again, understandably still worried about the bombing. She wanted to make sure everything was all right now, and before getting off the phone, she again urged him—as she'd done often in recent weeks—to consider leaving Iraq for good. As if he wasn't already aware of it, she frantically reminded him that she couldn't take it anymore, that she wanted to raise their family in a better place. "I just want to enjoy a peaceful night for once, Adnan. Baghdad isn't safe," she said, her final words before she hung up.

Adnan was torn apart by it all. If it wasn't for his shop, he would have left a long time ago, as it was becoming painfully obvious that the tumultuous situation in Baghdad was going to require years, maybe even a decade, before it would calm down.

He walked around his shop, looking at it from left to right. While he recalled happy memories, they were far from the current reality. He had been working there for the past forty-one years. His father had started the business in 1944, and when Adnan turned six, his father began bringing him along to help him carry books and rearrange them. As the years passed, Adnan realized that he had as much passion for the work and the store as his father did. He eventually took over the shop, and it had been his second home ever since. Come to think of it, he spent more time there than at home, but he had a family of his own now, a beautiful wife and two young boys, and their safety was not negotiable. *That's it. This bomb was the last straw,* he decided. He'd been thinking it over for several hours, in fact, and finally his mind was made up. "I'll organize the bookshop and sell it so we can start a new life elsewhere, in a new and better place," he said out loud, as if making a vow to no one in particular.

Adnan knew selling wouldn't be difficult, as his store was in the path of much traffic and a bevy of loyal customers, and anyone willing to take the daily risks of life would make some good money with the place.

Around six p.m., Adnan asked his assistant to leave. He needed to be alone. He turned off the front lights, put the CLOSED sign on the door, locked the shop up, and began rearranging books and putting them in the right sections. The Arabic ones were arranged according to subjects, and the English and other foreign language books were on the other side. Adnan's father was one of the first people to bring non-Arabic books to Baghdad. In addition to selling the books, Adnan's store also loaned them out. In one small sitting corner, patrons could read the books right there in the shop; his mother used to call it "the elderly corner," since the neighborhood elders dropped by daily to read and to have their morning tea with Adnan's father while making small talk.

Adnan finished putting every book back in its place. Then, with his hands in his pockets and sadness and grief in his eyes, he stared around at the place. "Is this it? Am I really going to abandon you?" he mumbled to himself, looking at the books.

Then, as if an answer to his question, reality struck him again. He recalled the ominous *BOOM*! of the last bomb, the image of people running and glass flying everywhere while he stood there in the chaos, surrounded by books.

"Right. There's no other way," he said in a louder voice, forming the words with his brain while his heart was crying out in agony.

Adnan thought about what life might have in store for him and his family if they left. *Will I be able to open a new shop somewhere, or will I have to start from scratch? Will the children be able to adjust? Will my wife love our new* home? There were questions, questions, and more questions flooding his mind, but Adnan had few answers.

What made things worse was that there were laws in place that forbade the shipping of large quantities of books from one country to another. Many approvals and permits had to be filed, and that meant Adnan would have to buy a new supply of books if he wanted to continue doing what he loved to do—the only job he knew. Buying new books and arranging them wouldn't be much of a hassle, since he'd have plenty of money from selling his store. It would only take some effort for that problem to be solved. What really pained Adnan, the toughest part, was having to let go of the books in the far right corner of his shop, the masterpieces. Those tomes were all rare, unique books, most more than fifty years old. They weren't even for sale because they were his treasures, and he considered them priceless. That private collection was very close to his heart, just as they had been to his father's. Anyone who wanted to read them had to ask days ahead of time and could only read them in the store; none of those books ever left the four walls of his bookstore, not even in the hands of his closest, most trusted friends or relatives. Unfortunately, the modern generation didn't seem to appreciate Adnan's treasures, so the corner hadn't seen much action for a long time, and the 300-plus books or so were all dusty.

Adnan had read more than half of them, but even he had neglected them for the last three or four years. Of course, this was not out of his own will, but because daily problems had impacted his life and eaten up all his spare time. Adnan moved to the corner where they sat, stood in front of them, and took a whiff, enjoying the ancient, almost musty aroma of those old pages. He moved closer and picked each book up and carefully cleaned their covers and bindings. He knew he could make a good fortune off of those books by selling them to some curator or collector, but those who would truly value the books had either left the country or were dealing with other priorities that left them little spending money for anything as frivolous as rare and beautiful books.

Nevertheless, they deserved to be dusted, for they were hidden gems.

After nearly two hours of dusting and thumbing through some of his inventory, Adnan was in the third row when a book fell. He quickly picked it up, and he could tell from the title that it was French. *Funny. I don't remember seeing this one before.* Out of curiosity, he opened the book. As is usually the case for books, the first page contained the name of the publisher and the copyright information. It was clearly mentioned that the work had been published in 1931. Intrigued, Adnan turned a few pages. Suddenly, something fell out of the book. When he carefully placed the book back on the shelf and bent down to see what it was, Adnan realized it was a small, leaf-shaped, locket. The pendant was dark golden in color, and two green stones, emeralds in the shape of eyes, were embedded in it.

With the most delicate of touches, Adnan opened the locket. On one side were the letters M&A, clearly engraved, but what caught Adnan's attention at once was what was on the other side: a black and white photograph of a woman behind a small glass. He quickly dusted it off. Although the photo wasn't that clear, the woman in the picture looked like a foreigner; she had light hair and features far different from most Arabic women. Still, her eyes were very beautiful and big, and her smile was innocent. In fact, Adnan had never seen such beautiful, wide eyes. She was indeed a very nice-looking woman, but something told Adnan she harbored some sadness beneath that pretty grin. "Who was this woman?" Adnan asked himself.

He continued staring at the photo, studying it for a few minutes. He brought it very close to his eyes, then held it a bit further away, as if to see if there was more to it, something he'd missed. At the same time, he kept on asking himself the same question: "Who are you? Do I know you?

When the locket returned no answers, he put it in his pocket and picked up the French book from the shelf. In spite of his efforts to handle it with care and turn the pages gently, the entire inside of the book fell out of its cover, as if it wasn't attached to the binding at all. Adnan stopped, surprised to see that the original inside pages of the book had been replaced with paper of a very different color. Everything was handwritten in English, not printed from a press, in spite of the publisher's name in the front. Adnan's heart began to beat faster as he flipped through the pages. The words were scribed in black ink, all English, with the exception of a few Arabic words scattered throughout here and there.

A sudden rush of adrenaline ran through Adnan. His face began to sweat, and, full of excitement, he took the pendant out of his pocket. He held it in his right hand and kept the book in his left. Then, with fast feet, he made his way to his desk. He removed everything from his desk and carefully placed his new discoveries in front of him. He looked at his watch and impatiently dialed his wife; fortunately, she answered after a couple of rings. "I won't be home tonight," he said. "Don't worry. I just have some extra work to do in the shop and a few things to fix if I'm going to have to sell the place."

While his wife didn't like to hear that he wouldn't be home, she was very glad to hear that he'd finally made his mind up. She knew better than to bicker with him about not coming home, as she didn't want him to change his mind again, after all the time it had taken her to convince him to leave. She took it as good news, more than enough, and quickly told him goodnight and got off the phone.

Adnan opened the locket again and placed it on its side so the lady's face was toward him. He then opened the first page of the book.

The date was written on the top in Arabic, July 12, 1958. Adnan took a deep breath and started reading the book: "I have a feeling things won't go well when we return to Baghdad tomorrow..."

I am writing this so my beautiful daughter knows the sacrifices her mother and I have made in the name of our love. If I'm not there to tell my daughter who her father is, this will help her a lot—or at least I hope so.

I was born in 1934 in Diyala, an only child to my parents and the light and joy in their lives. My father, along with my two uncles, had inherited a large plot from their late father. It was beautiful agricultural land, with soil so rich that everything they planted turned into gold. My father and uncles were fond of their work and took care of the land very well, and our farms supplied fruits and vegetables to many areas across the country.

I had a happy childhood. I enjoyed watching my father and uncles do their daily work at the farm, and my mother and my uncles' wives laughed as they went about their daily chores, whether it was cooking or helping the men with some farm work. I loved running around those green farms, collecting dates, oranges, and grapes and playing with my younger cousins. I was particularly close to Mustafa, who was only four months younger.

I will never forget the good times we had. Every day, just before sunrise, Mustafa and I used to run to the end of the farm, to a little hut my late grandfather had built years earlier. We'd climb up on top of it and watch the sunflowers open up while the sun was rising. How beautiful a sight it was! We just watched and watched, and everything in life seemed so simple, so perfect. I remember racing him all the way back. We played games like hide-and-seek and football, but the thing Mustafa loved most was climbing that high palm tree next to the house. He loved playing up there, and he never lost to me once when we raced to climb it. He was quick as a bullet, and I'd bet my life that nobody in Iraq could climb it faster than him. With several moves, he was up the tree, picking the sweetest date, while I was still struggling halfway through. It was a lovely, peaceful life till, out of nowhere, a tragedy hit.

On a rainy day in February of 1943, we received shocking news. My father and one of my uncles were on their way to Baghdad via public transportation, a small, twelve-passenger local bus, the only one in the province that went to Baghdad daily at that time, always at seven a.m. sharp. That day, the roads were muddy and dangerous. It had rained all night before, and the rain continued even after they'd left home. They were urged by my mother and my aunt to delay their visit, but they insisted that they go, stating that they had urgent meetings to attend. In the end, that decision would prove to be a fatal one, but I learned early in life that you can't fight fate. That day was to be their calling day, that bus ride their last.

Witnesses recalled that a commuting van slid from one of the bridges just outside Baghdad and dropped, headfirst, into the Tigris River. The incident resulted in seven casualties, and my father and uncle were among them. They passed away instantly.

The shock hit us hard. My mother was hurt the most, as she was an orphan herself and had no brothers or sisters. My father was her everything, so she was devastated. She'd finally found someone to love in life, but he was taken away from her in a heartbeat. Before that, she'd always worn the most beautiful smile, but I never saw it again after that day.

After the tragedy, my youngest uncle was in charge of all of us. It wasn't easy for such a young man to take care of three families and manage all the farms by himself, so my cousin Mustafa and I tried to help. After all, we were the oldest of the children, both a ripe, old age of ten. I always told Mustafa we had a short-lived childhood, and we were men before our time.

I loved working on the farm and helping out, but Mustafa only did it because he felt obliged to. Nevertheless, once school was out, we both helped with everything from seeding and irrigation to driving the tractors, the best part of all. At that age, I had four things in my life: my mother, Mustafa, the rest of the family, and the farm.

Ten months later, life struck me with another harsh blow, when my mother passed away from pneumonia. The doctors tried to help, but they were of little use. She hadn't been the same since my father's untimely death, and she didn't seem to have the will to live anymore.

So, I was an orphan before I even turned eleven. From that day on, I dedicated everything to my work. I put my heart and soul into it and was my uncle's right arm. He taught me everything, and as years passed, I began to take on many responsibilities of the farm, lightening his load a great deal.

As difficult as it was to study, since there were only a few schools within a thirty-miles radius, my father had always insisted that learning was a priority. I finished primary school, but I dropped out after that. With my parents gone, I had no desire to continue my education. Besides, I poured all my attention and energy into our farm, taking care of the land that belonged to my uncle and used to belong to my father.

One day, when I was fourteen, I was in Baghdad, waiting for my uncle near a busy market. I saw a well-dressed Iraqi gentleman in a black suit and shiny black shoes. He looked to be in his early forties, with fairly dark skin; big, dark brown eyes; an impeccably trimmed mustache; and a medium build and height. He was speaking English, talking to a British gentleman, and both of them laughed heartily every once in a while. I watched them for several moments, as I was mesmerized by the man's personality, looks, and manner of speaking. He was so elegant, so confident. I was impressed, and I felt something I still can't explain. At that moment, I wished I was like him, elegant and able to talk articulately and confidently, just enjoying myself.

I gave in to my strong urge to approach him. I greeted the men and shook their hands. I made sure to tell the Iraqi that I admired him because he looked so elegant, and I asked him where he'd learned to speak English so well.

With a warm smile I won't forget, he tapped me on the back and asked for my name. "And what brings you to this market today, my boy?" he said.

"I am Ali. We have several farms in Diyala, and my relatives and I take care of them. My uncle and I come here from time to time for our business," I replied.

"That's nice, Ali. I'm Radhi, an engineer. I know English because I studied in the United Kingdom," he said, with warmth oozing from his voice. He'd answered me, a random kid on the street, even though he didn't have to, and I was amazed how kind he was to me, right from the start.

After his answer, I was still curious, and he seemed to sense that. Radhi took me aside, bent down to my eye level, and asked me if I would like to learn English. I nodded excitedly. I'd never thought about it before, but I desired to be able to speak like him with people from other lands.

He smiled and pulled me closer and said, "To learn English, you must first know how to read and write Arabic, young Ali"

I told him I'd finished primary school and that I knew how to read and write Arabic and that my uncle and his wife wrote and read it very well. He told me that was a good start, and then he let go of my hand, straightened himself up, and asked me to meet him the very next day, same time and place. He assured me I wouldn't be disappointed.

When my uncle came back, I told him about my encounter with Mr. Radhi and begged him to let me stay for another day in Baghdad to meet him again. Much to my delight, he allowed me to stay.

At precisely the same time the following day, in the exact same spot, Mr. Radhi showed up, as promised. He was carrying a small box of books, which he handed to me. "Ali, four of these books will help you learn English. Read them little by little. The last book, the bigger one with the green leather cover, is an encyclopedia about plants, gardening, and farming. You will need to study them well, but before you take this step, before you embark on the new language, you have to promise me that you will master Arabic, that your uncle and aunt will teach you well."

I was extremely happy. I thanked him so many times, with tears in my eyes.

He took out his handkerchief wiped my tears and told me that if I needed more books, I could look for them in the Al Aadhamiya area, there was a good shop there. He also told me that if I ever needed any help, I could ask anyone in the Safina area about him.

My life suddenly had more meaning. I continued helping on the farms, and at the same time, I read as much as I could. As the years passed, my younger cousins grew and got more involved.

Mustafa, on the other hand, couldn't have been more distanced. His passion wasn't farming, and the only thing he liked about nature and the outdoors was climbing that palm tree. He wanted to travel, to go as far away as possible. He was always telling me that he wanted to go to Basra, to the port to be more specific, where he could get involved in trading and learn from the best there. His desire was to travel away with the vessels and discover new places, and a few years later, he finally left. He was only sixteen, so his father wasn't so keen on the idea, but as painful as it was for him to let his son go, he didn't want to get in the way of his desire.

My uncle had a friend in Basra who would serve as an excellent guide for Mustafa in the beginning. He also gave him some money that would help him settle in. For the first few weeks after my cousin and friend left for Basra, I felt lonely. He was, after all, my best friend. Suddenly, the person I shared almost everything with wasn't there anymore. To comfort myself, I took solace in my books, and I dug deeper and deeper into reading.

Whenever I went to Baghdad, I returned with a book or two. I became fluent in English by reading the books over and over again. For hours at night, I read in the warm glow of the candle next to my bed, and waking up every morning with a book in my hand became normal.

After I gained a decent command of the language, I decided to study the encyclopedia about plants, the big green book Mr. Radhi had given me. Within a short period of time, I decided to put the advice in that book into practice. I made a small garden for myself, just outside my home, and began experimenting with whatever seeds I could get from my Baghdad acquaintances.

The more trials I did in my little garden, the better it became, and I gained so much experience along the way. I learned what to plant and when, and my continuous visits to Baghdad broadened my horizons even more. It was the perfect learning process, one that mingled with my imagination.

I loved Baghdad and found it to be a beautiful place full of kind people. There were newer, wider streets than any I'd seen anywhere else in Iraq, but there were also beautiful, narrow, old streets that seemed to transport me back through decades of time, revealing the city's heritage. There were palm trees everywhere, and I loved the bridges that linked the two sides of Baghdad together, over the beautiful Tigris River.  Just walking

15

beside the Tigris anytime of the day was rewarding for my mind and soul, each breath of air along it a lovely, invigorating treat for my nostrils.

The city was full of busy markets, and several vendors sold goods out of their wooden carriages. I learned quickly that whatever my heart desired could be found in Baghdad—everything from fresh fruit and vegetables to cattle, poultry, fish, spices, garments, clothes, antique furniture, and musical instruments. There was even a vast animal market where people could purchase pets or even weird, exotic animals like snakes and monkeys. The city was constantly buzzing with life, and I felt more alive each time I visited it.

It was quite the social scene. The city was bursting with cafés and restaurants, where elegantly dressed musicians, poets, journalists, and pedestrians gathered. Baghdad was Iraq's city that never slept. As late-night parties were wrapping up, some were preparing for their morning prayers in the hundreds or more beautiful mosques. The streets were never quiet.

I'd seen a lot of beautiful places over the years, but one was unforgettable—a particular spot along the Tigris River on the north side of the city. I'd first noticed it while walking along the river on a cold night in February. It was a large, empty area surrounded by an eight-foot-high fence of green-painted wood. There were no buildings on it, and the place seemed abandoned, as if it was unknown or forgotten by the rest of the vibrant city. After I saw it, I visited it every time I went to Baghdad, and not once did I see another soul there.

I wanted to learn more about the strange, alluring place. One day, I decided to climb the fence and check it out for myself. I knew it was wrong to trespass on land that wasn't mine and didn't necessarily belong to the public, but it was as if a strange voice was beckoning me, as if the land itself was crying out, complaining about the neglect it had suffered. Deep inside, I knew that the land deserved more attention than it was getting. I walked around the whole place, admiring its beautiful, untouched soil that felt moist when I picked it up and carried a rich, earthy aroma. I just sat there for an hour, lost deep in my thoughts. I planned what I would do with that land if it was mine, if I had the chance to use it for anything, and somehow, I knew I'd have an opportunity to put those plans into action someday.

On my following visits to Baghdad, I made some inquiries about the place. As it turned out, the land belonged to a Jewish Iraqi family that had left Iraq. Their only living relative in Baghdad wasn't at all interested in it and was ready to sell it. I knew it wouldn't be difficult to purchase the land from them, but I wanted to be sure I was making the right decision. I had to be certain, as well, that if I did decide to take on that new experience, to make that my true future and passion, my uncle would be all right with that. After all he'd done for me, I did not want to leave him shorthanded on my family's farms.

I was eighteen at that time, and for the past thirteen months, I'd worked very hard to teach my younger cousins everything I knew about farm work. We'd gone over every detail, no matter how small, and only after I felt sure and confident that they had learned all there was to know, I approached my uncle about my desire to leave and told him what I had in mind. I told him I wanted to sell my share of the land to the family and that I would gladly accept any price he came up with. After all, we were all from the same bloodline.

Naturally, my uncle was sad to hear that I was ready to leave, but he had watched me grow over the years, and he'd seen a change in me. All along, he'd been waiting for that day to come, the day when I'd be ready to venture out on my own. He'd seen the excitement in my eyes whenever I went with him to Baghdad, and he knew I was destined for something other than working on our family farms. Thus, when I broke the news to him, it didn't come as much of a surprise. He told me he knew it was only a matter of time and said he was sure I'd succeed in whatever I planned to do. He generously offered to pay more than my share of the family land was worth, stating that without me and all my hard work, the farms wouldn't have been so prosperous. He hugged me tightly and said, "You are always welcome here anytime you need to come back. This will always be your home, Ali."

With the money I got, I bought the amazing little patch of secluded land in a matter of weeks. I already had everything carefully organized in my head. I'd imagined it all the first time I'd seen the place, and I now just had to put all my thoughts and dreams in action.

I was going to make the best plant nursery in Baghdad, something Baghdad had never had before. I wanted to create something people would talk about, a place people would like to visit as well as buy from, and I knew just the person to help me achieve those lofty goals. I would contact the same person who'd helped me find my passion and opened that new path in my life in the first place, Mr. Radhi.

Finding Mr. Radhi was very easy, as everyone in the areas he mentioned knew him. He was a well-respected figure in society, one of the few Iraqi civil engineers who'd graduated in the UK at that time, and he was also close to one of the members of the royal family, in spite of his loathing of politics.

While walking to his place, I wondered if he'd even remember me. It had been four years since he'd given me those books, the volumes that changed my life forever and opened a new world to me. I reached his home just after noon. It was near the water, surrounded by beautiful villas. Mr. Radhi's villa was right on the riverfront, just 100 feet away from the Tigris, separated from the roaring river only by a small street used by commuters and cars as well. There was a short, off-white gate and a black door. The whole house could be seen clearly from outside.

I knocked twice and waited, and just when I was about to knock a third time, an old man greeted me. He was well dressed, sporting a black suit and a crisp, perfectly ironed white shirt. He spoke in a low voice, and I assumed he was in charge of household security. I introduced myself and asked for Mr. Radhi, and the old man informed me that the man I sought wouldn't be back for an hour. He told me I should return then, but I explained to him that I had traveled a very long way and would prefer to wait there for him. The kind, understanding man opened the gates and invited me to sit in the garden.

Mr. Radhi's garden was huge and stretched all across the front of the villa. It was home to many colorful flowers, a few palm trees, and a fairly green lawn, though there were some yellowed patches. Overall it was a decent garden, though not as spectacular as I would have expected. With a minute of observation, I'd already envisioned how I could turn the space into an absolute paradise.

The house was lovely on the outside, a large, three-level home constructed out of white and off-white stones. The floor of the entrance was fashioned from beautiful fading orange marble. The façade that looked out over the river was equipped with eight windows, four of them reaching from the floor to the ceiling. It was obvious that Mr. Radhi was a lover of light—sunlight in particular.

Around one p.m., I heard a car approaching. When the horn honked twice, the old man moved quickly and opened the gate, and a black car entered. Mr. Radhi was sitting in the back, still wearing that dapper-looking hat and sunglasses.

As soon as he got out of the car, he looked over and noticed me sitting in the garden. The old man whispered a few words in his ear, and Mr. Radhi handed his bag to the driver and started walking toward me.

"Can I do something for you, young man?" Mr. Radhi asked in Arabic as he neared.

I replied in near-perfect English, "I'm sure you can, Mr. Radhi."

He was a few feet away and looked at me for a second. Then, a big smile crept over his face, and he said, "Ali, is that you?"

I gave him a slight nod.

"You have grown into a handsome man! I always believed I'd see you again someday, and this is a pleasant surprise indeed. You must be starving. Come inside, and we'll have lunch," he said, patting me on the back.

The interior of the house was extremely beautiful, with class written all over it. Rustic, antique silk carpets were stretched all over the floors, and the walls were adorned with long, silver-framed mirrors and beautiful paintings. The furnishings included two beautiful green fabric sofas, and crystal chandeliers hung from the ceiling. I'd seen quite a few houses in my life, but never had I seen any so elegant. The rosewood tables were exquisite, covered with hand-knitted, soft cloths; I had never felt anything so smooth before.

Amidst all that rich, artistic beauty, what I admired the most was the meter-and-a-half-tall grandfather clock in the corner. It was fashioned from dark cherry wood, hand-carved with golden angels dancing in the sky, overlooking a festive feast. Amazed, I instantly asked Mr. Radhi about it, and he told me he'd bought the clock from England a few years back. The delicate hand carvings were made by a student of David

Roentgen, a well-known German Rococo cabinet- and clockmaker. "The wood's the best you'll find anywhere, and the mechanics are absolutely fascinating. It weighs more than a hundred pounds," he said. "You'd need a real sharp axe to break it!"

"Oh, but I'd never want to break anything so beautiful," I said with a smile.

After I took some time to admire that room and all of its masterpieces, Mr. Radhi showed me around some other rooms, each with its own identity. When we finally entered the dining room, lunch was already being served.

We were soon joined by a woman, and Mr. Radhi introduced her as his wife, Laila. She was a very elegant lady, rather tall, with long, beautiful, black hair that cascaded down over her shoulders like an ebony waterfall. She had light blue eyes that seemed to glisten, but her most striking features were her prominent cheekbones and her small, straight nose. Her skin was much fairer in complexion than Mr. Radhi's, but they were a perfect match, both in their forties, no more a year or so apart. I could sense their deep connection immediately, and it was clear that they belonged to each other.

We enjoyed the food and conversation for more than two hours. I learned that the couple had only had one child, but he'd died at the age of five, due to fever. I could still see the sadness in Madam Laila's eyes whenever she talked about their son; coincidently, his name was the same as mine, Ali.

After our delicious and friendly lunch, Mr. Radhi took me to his study, a small, square, cozy room decorated with brown leather armchairs and a small, round table. There were shelves on all four walls, full of books, and on top of the shelves in the center wall was a glass-encased saying by the Prophet Muhammad: "Go in quest of knowledge, even unto China."

When Mr. Radhi saw me staring at those words, he said, "Ali, there is nothing better than learning. I have learned all my life and I will continue to do so." He then talked a bit about his book collection and explained where the books had come from. After that, he asked me to join him in the garden so he could have a smoke of his pipe; his lovely wife didn't like him smoking inside their lovely home.

In the garden, we talked for hours. Mr. Radhi showed genuine interest in hearing everything about my life. I started from the beginning and told him all that had happened to me up to that point, everything I could recall about my life leading up to that moment. I explained how I'd lost my parents and told him about the hard but rewarding work on our farms for all those years. I talked about my passion for agriculture, nurturing plants, and farming. I also made sure to mention the influence he'd had on me the day I'd met him in the old market. "You opened my eyes that day," I said. "You showed me that my life could hold adventures I never expected." I then told him I'd bought a nice plot of land near the river in the northern part of the city. "It's not a huge piece of land," I said, "but it's big enough for what

I've got in mind. I can set up my nursery there, and I want it to be unlike any other place in Baghdad." I was very excited about my new mission in life, and he allowed me to go on and on without interruptions, until I finally stopped.

All his words seemed wise, but this time, he uttered some I'd never forget: "Ali, I am confident it will be special, and I'm ready to help you however I can. I will design a house for you there and supervise its construction. Also, my house is always open to you, and you may consider all my books yours, if you need to learn more about anything"

For the next few months, I worked together with Mr. Radhi and the laborers he'd hired. In exactly four months, everything was ready. My small house, complete with a climbing vine, was built in the far end corner that led to the river. It had a living room, a bedroom, a tiny kitchen, and two bathrooms. The little garden ended at the river, and I had a small wooden boat yard there so I could take a ride in my small boat whenever I felt compelled to. In the front was a nursery, cultivated for growing roses, tulips, jasmine, and other flowers. The flowerbed stretched from the main entrance to the corners, where palms and citrus trees grew in neat arrangements. There was a small sitting area positioned in front of a beautiful fountain, with two angels playing music in the center of it all. All of this was surrounded by a quaint fence, and the place was a heaven all its own.

Mr. Radhi refused to accept any payment for the work, so in exchange; I offered to redesign his garden for him. When he agreed, I asked him to give me a week to finish the layout I had in mind and several months to follow through with the plans. I already had great plans in mind for his garden, and I knew exactly how I thought it should be. It was a wonderful space, and I could picture lovely outdoor sitting areas there, where Mr. Radhi, his wife, and their guests could enjoy the surrounding natural beauty I had planned for it.

It was simple enough to go on instinct for what colors and types of flowers and trees would work best. It was my first chance to put my years of farm experience to the test, and I was confident I would succeed.

Mr. Radhi's house was designed without gardens outside the gates, so I had to make the best of what rested behind them. I wanted each garden I designed to have its own special identity, I didn't like the idea of open gardens. After all, it wasn't a public park that just anyone could walk into. I wanted Mr. Radhi's garden and any others I worked on to lure visitors in with its beauty. To me, the garden wasn't an object; rather, it was as much a living thing as any human, and it had the right to express itself however it chose. Just like a house, I believed the garden should have its own privacy and an entrance.

I decided I would give the garden two entrances, one at the front, close to the main entrance, and the second at the far end, for those coming from inside the house. I selected four ficus trees, two to be placed at each garden entrance. They were a meter high and trimmed into round shapes, though they could be shaped differently in the future. The outer path around the garden was a foot wide, a mixture of small, shiny, white and black stones. Next to it were pink and white roses, neatly planted in two straight, parallel lines. The middle of the garden was an extravaganza of colors—yellow, red, and blue. Tulips, a large mixture of white and red roses, white orchids, and some lilies were all selected carefully to portray a message of appreciation for life, something I felt Mr. Radhi and Madam Laila had within them but had neglected a bit in their garden. I also planted six small cycads in various places, and each was surrounded by a bed of purple tulips. I'd always thought a garden should tickle more than the eyes; it had to alter all the human senses, and I knew the gardenia could do just that. Thus, I planted four beds at each end, and the flowers were so fragrant that their scent could be enjoyed from across the street.

Madam Laila was extremely fascinated and joyfully grateful for the work I'd done outside their home. She was impressed with the flower selections and the colors, and she said, "This is a piece of art, worthy of a portrait!"

The garden had to be carefully maintained, so I taught their gardener what to do and when to do it. As the weeks passed, the garden just bloomed and blossomed into more and more beauty.

A neighbor stopped by and praised it, and others followed. In fact, many of their neighbors used afternoon tea with Madam Laila as an excuse to get a peek at the place. When the word spread about Mr. Radhi's garden, Madam Laila insisted that they have a party so they could invite all their friends and even some royalty and show them the garden everyone had been talking about. For me, business began to boom.

The preparations for the get-together took over a week. It was the first party they'd hosted in years, and when the day finally came, it was one of those parties the people of Baghdad talked about for several weeks. Madam Laila had arranged everything in the villa. It looked even more spectacular with all the decorations. Everything absolutely sparkled. She'd selected the very best plates and cutlery, and the food selection was extravagant. Appetizers, both cold and hot, would be served throughout the evening. A wide variety of main courses was masterfully chosen, over twenty vegetable, chicken, meat, and fish dishes, all freshly prepared in different culinary styles. Mr. Radhi bought a large red carpet to welcome his guests at the main gate, and I took care of the garden, adding the trimmings and final, delicate touches to make it even more breathtaking.

The guests were the elite of Baghdad. Over forty families showed up, including doctors, lawyers, teachers, musicians, businessmen, and several ambassadors. Most had some influence in Baghdad society, but the main guest was one of the king's far cousins. When her highness walked in, there was a moment of silence. She was extremely elegant, with beautiful, long hair that flowed down her smooth shoulders. She was wearing a red dress with several layers of gorgeous, rich fabric. Her slender neck was adorned with a long string of pearls.

She was known for her beauty, yet she was very humble and kind to everyone.

Madam Laila introduced her to all the guests, then proudly took her on a tour of their home, taking time to describe the many paintings Mr. Radhi had purchased at an auction in London a few months prior. Laila then escorted her esteemed guest outside, where she took her on a stroll through the glorious garden. Madam Laila was very thorough in describing every detail, and she made sure to tell her all about the plants, where they were originally from and the best time of the year to grow them. She also mentioned the special care each and every one of them needed. The day before the party, I had taught Madam Laila everything she needed to know about the garden, and she was a quick learner. Her highness was impressed with the garden and complimented Madam Laila on its beauty. She asked who had done the work, and Laila gladly gave me credit.

The day before, both Mr. Radhi and Madam Laila had asked me to be involved with the guests and explain everything to them, but I told them I wasn't quite ready to mingle with them. I apologized and explained that I'd never been around that type of crowd and wasn't yet confident enough. I assured them, though, that I'd be close by; I didn't want to miss any of the action—not for anything in the world. I wanted to see the party from a bird's-eye view, so I asked Mr. Radhi if I could sit on the upper floor and watch from the windows. He agreed, so I positioned myself there during the party and opened the windows a bit so I could hear what everyone was talking about. I'd never felt so much pride and happiness as I did when all the people in the elegant clothes began talking about the work I'd done in the garden. They gushed about the colors of the roses, the tulip locations, and the designs I'd created by meticulously selecting and trimming the perfect trees. So many compliments were made about the picturesque garden that I began to feel like the party was a celebration in my honor.

The most common question was who was behind the work in the garden and how long the work took. Mr. Radhi and Madam Laila were more than happy to tell them all about it. I knew then that my work would be very sought-after. I'd have to get better at it, as I'd have a large and very important group of clientele to please. I would need more help and a greater variety of plants and flowers. I wanted each garden to be unique in every way, each design to be more and more creative. I knew I could achieve my dreams and make a big name for myself in Baghdad; perhaps even in all of Iraq, just by doing an excellent job at the gardening that was my passion.

After finishing their evening tea and enjoying themselves immensely, the guests began to leave. I had made sure there would be a bouquet of flowers for each of the departing families, the perfect friendly touch to end a lovely evening.

When the last guests left and Mr. Radhi and Madam Laila sat down to relax in the garden, I joined them. I thanked them a lot, for I was a bit overwhelmed from the joy the day had brought. Much to my surprise, though, Madam Laila thanked me.

She pulled me into a hug and uttered flattering words that still often ring in my ears: "Ali, thank you. Your presence and your garden has brought life back to us, back to this house. You can't imagine how long we have needed that."

Mr. Radhi had some kind words of his own to share. He looked at me straight in the eyes and said, "Don't thank us for anything. From the first moment you came to me in the market years ago, when you approached me so confidently, I sensed something about you. I felt that you were different somehow. You just needed a push. The talent and determination were already within you. We only helped pave the way, made people notice how uniquely talented you are. I'm sure you will do great things and make us proud. You're the same age as my son would have been, and you are like a son to us." He then held me tight to him and continued, "You are *our* Ali, but to the rest, you will be The Gardener of Baghdad! Let's have some cake and tea and enjoy this delightful evening and the full moon, shall we?"

We sat there for another hour, laughing and talking. It was a moment of my life that I wanted to capture in my memory, a blessed gathering that I would always cherish, especially since so many hardworking days were about to come my way...

# Chapter 2

Just when Adnan was about to turn the next page of the handwritten memoir hidden inside the cover of a French book, the electricity went off. It wasn't all that out of the ordinary and was part of everyday life in conflict-torn, modern-day Baghdad. It was so common, in fact, that people were more surprised when the electricity stayed on than they were when it went off. Electricity was a rare luxury, a shy, occasionally visiting guest who only dropped by for a quick greeting and was always quick to leave again.

The place went completely dark, as it was very late and far past closing hours. Adnan decided there was no point in firing up the backup generator. It was a commercial area, and being the only shop with lights on at that hour would only draw attention—not a smart move for security reasons. There was no way he would go out into the dark streets to head home, and besides that, he was far too immersed in the story in the book. He simply had to continue reading. The allure of the story was so powerful, for it had transported him to a long-forgotten era in Baghdad, before there was so much turmoil and political unrest tearing the people's lives and the scenic city apart.

Adnan was in dire need of a cigarette, but unlike most places in Baghdad, his store allowed no smoking; this was due, in part, to his desire to protect the brittle, old, very flammable pages of his precious books. He took out his pack of cigarettes, opened the door, and lit one. He blew wisps of smoke out the door as he looks out at the dark, empty streets. Adnan tried to picture how Baghdad must have looked to Ali's eyes, more than fifty years ago. He imagined it would have been safer, more alive back then, when people could walk the streets and enjoy one another and the view. He wondered who Ali, The Gardener of Baghdad, really was. *How did this book get here anyway?* Adnan pondered. *Did my father even know it was here?* Questions swarmed through his head as he quickly finished his smoking break, taking one deep inhale after another. As soon as his cigarette was safely out, he walked back inside, locked the front door, and retrieved several candles from the front desk. He made himself comfortable in his favorite leather chair again and continued reading. "Starting the day after Mr. Radhi's party, my nursery became busy..."

꙳꙳꙳

People began flocking in from all over. Many bought flowers, and some purchased trees and seeds of various types. Some even wanted to do their whole gardens all over again.

32

I was extremely busy, and my business couldn't have been better. I'd hired two helpers, and we managed to keep everything under control. I was glad I'd created a sitting area around the fountain, as people seemed to enjoy resting there with their friends and family while they drank tea and waited for us to fulfill their orders.

We worked six days a week. On Saturdays, my off days, I often had lunch at Mr. Radhi's house. I began to feel like a real part of their family, and I enjoyed talking to them. I learned much from Mr. Radhi about a variety of topics, and I read many of the books he suggested. I looked up to him and his wife as my surrogate parents, of sorts, and I was their Ali.

During my workdays, I usually spent my evenings at cafés, enjoying the talk of the town with the locals. There was nothing better than smoking a water pipe and enjoying a cup of tea after a hard day's work. I spent nights reading a book at home, sitting in the garden, or having a drink and a bite to eat at the local restaurants, enjoying the great voices of the many musicians the great city was known for.

Time flew by, and before I even realized it, a year had passed since I'd left my uncle's farm. During that time, I'd seen my uncle only a few times. He was very proud of what I had achieved, and I was happy to hear that everything at the farm was in good, working order and that my cousins had kept up with their tasks and chores.

One day, my uncle came to visit, and he had a bright look on his face. He looked happier than I'd seen him looking in a year as he announced, "Ali, I have a surprise. Look who's here!"

Then, all of the sudden, Mustafa stepped out from behind his father. My cousin and childhood best friend had grown up. He was dressed in fancy clothes, a fine-looking, tall man, though he had the same sharp eyes and naturally straight eyebrows. He had grown a thin mustache, but the most significant change was his hair. His black mane was carefully combed to one side, and it made him look more serious than Ali remembered. He gave me the same nice smile I remembered, and we embraced one another tightly. The three of us talked for hours before my uncle left, and Mustafa stayed with me for the next few days.

I'd heard scattered news about his progress over the years, and I'd received a few letters from him, but I was eager to hear about all he'd been up to. Mustafa told me all about his past four years, where he'd started and where he'd ended up. As I listened, I realized he'd had somewhat of a rough start. He first worked in Basra, a city in southern Iraq. He said Basra still had a nightlife comparable to Baghdad's, and it was known for its delicious seafood. At first, he worked at the main port, carrying goods from vessel to deck, a job his father's friend managed to get for him. After a few months, he joined a crew that traveled with a spice trader. He went as far east as India and to parts of Africa in the west. He'd seen many strange things on his voyages, things very different from our culture. "There are some things out there you would never understand, Ali," he said. He

34

learned much from and about other people who had other habits and beliefs, but the thing he loved to learn about most was precious stones.

In his second year traveling the ocean, in a port in southern India, he met an old trader who was involved with those commodities. The two became very close, and they ran into each other quite often, a couple times in Africa and several in India. Mustafa learned a lot about the old Indian trader, who knew everything there was to know about precious stones and gems. He'd dealt with hundreds of them, some worth a fortune. Mustafa loved learning from him, as he was a master in trading and knew his business well. Once Mustafa felt he could trust the man, he began to work with him, bit by bit. After a few years of good fortune and trade, and with the help and blessing of his Indian mentor, Mustafa had gained the experience and wealth he needed to be successful. Mustafa secured his own vessel and crew. It wasn't a large ship, but it was adequate for his work. He had all the contacts, resources, and skills he needed, and he was doing well.

All of Mustafa's weird encounters during his travels sounded like an adventure novel to me. He'd seen king cobras, monkeys, elephants, huge temples, beautiful lakes and markets, bizarre cultural dancing, and festivals. His tales were fascinating, and I hung on every word. We laughed when he told me that he'd eaten some food that was so spicy it made his teeth burn and left him feeling sick for days. Until then, I hadn't realized just how much I'd missed Mustafa. I'd been so busy for the past year, so engaged in my work and trying to make everything perfect. His visit was a much-needed relief from the stress, and he showed up at just the right time. Even after all that time apart, the two of us shared a special bond that could ease all the troubles away.

I told him what had happened with me and showed him what I had done and where my plans were headed. He was very impressed and proud, and he assured me that I was destined for success.

We had many laughs, but our conversation gradually became more businesslike and professional. Since he was a bit of a world traveler, I asked him about places I could visit, as I wanted to expand my business and bring in new plants and seeds from India, Ceylon, and tropical regions in Africa, exotic plants that had never lived in Baghdad before, like some of those I'd seen in the green, leather-bound book Mr. Radhi had given me. Mustafa promised that he'd gather information for me and would return in two months with a nice voyage planned out for me. He thought it was a wise idea for me to visit other places, to get a better feel of what was out there in the world, and I was excited to experience and study different places, to go on adventures like he had and bring back the plants of the world to introduce them to the gardens and people of Baghdad.

I'd envied Mr. Radhi's suave, debonair looks the very first day I'd seen him in the market, and as I began to meet doctors and businessmen daily, that desire to carry myself that way grew into a necessity. I had grown confident in myself and in my work, and I felt it was time for me to dress professionally. If I was going to travel abroad, I wanted to make a solid impression on those I met. When I asked Mr. Radhi for help, he sent me to his tailor. I had several suits made and chose a Faisaliya hat to accompany them, a special hat worn by Iraqis and specifically by Baghdadis. I learned that the hat got its name from the first king, Faisal, who desired a hat with a uniquely Iraqi identity. To give my outfit its own unique flare, I always attached a rose to my suit, a different color every day. When Madam Laila first saw me in one of my suits, she proudly wept. Everyone talked about how stylish I looked, and they seemed to notice that I'd looked after every detail of my appearance, right down to picking the most perfect, most beautiful roses for my colorful boutonnières.

As promised, Mustafa returned two months later, with a list of places and people that he thought I should visit. He'd met them all before, and while I was worried about the language barrier, Mustafa assured me that most of them spoke English. He said some even knew a bit of Arabic, and he joked, "Just use your hands, and you'll do pretty well!"

I had also asked Mustafa to find a lovely ruby ring that I could give to Madam Laila as a gift for all she'd done for me. When I gave it to her, she promised she'd never take it off.

I had never traveled outside Iraq before, and it took time to get my passport, but with the help of some of Mr. Radhi's influential contacts, it worked out well in the end. I was away for three weeks, and my two

37

assistants took very good care of my business while I was gone.

As Mustafa had promised, the experience was indeed unique. I couldn't believe only a thousand miles could make such a difference in cultures and ways of life. Everything was different, from buildings to religion to food. What I loved most was the landscape. Unfortunately, I was always in a hurry and didn't seem to have enough time to enjoy everything I wanted to see, but my visits were still quite beneficial. I found just what I'd gone looking for, and I made several agreements for the continuous supply of new seeds and trees that would take my nursery to a whole new level. Thanks to Mustafa's advice and travel plans, everything went smoothly, and I was back in no time.

I made sure to spread the word about all the wonderful new plants I had available, and I asked Madam Laila to send word to her highness, the one that was present at the party a while back. Just a few days later, I received a request to deliver three plants to the king's palace, and I was thrilled and honored.

When I was chosen to design the landscape for one of Baghdad's new squares, where the meetings of the Baghdad Pact Assembly would be held, I knew I'd been accepted as the people's gardener, The Gardener of Baghdad. The Baghdad Pact was sponsored by the United States of America and Great Britain and was meant to oppose the spread of the Soviet Union. A northern wall would be built, with the blessing of Iran, Iraq, Turkey, Pakistan, and Britain. The pact was signed in Baghdad, where the headquarters remained. It took two days to design the square and select just the right flowers. It was an important day in Baghdad's history, and everything had to be perfect.

It looked absolutely brilliant on opening day, speckled with a rainbow of flowers. There were delicately trimmed trees, and five large palms were planted in the middle of the square in a circular shape; these represented the five members of the Assembly. The name of Baghdad, our fair city, was spelled out with red and white flowers on one of the borders, and the square looked like a piece of Heaven on Earth amidst the four intersecting roads. A delegation on behalf of the royal family and others congratulated me for a job well done, and all referred to me as The Gardener of Baghdad, much to my delight. Little did I know that the name would be remembered for something else, something entirely different from my beautiful garden designs…

✻✻✻

As I look at the love of my life, Mary, sleeping so quietly with our beautiful baby, our little Laila, our angel lying next to her, I remember the first day I met Mary. I have to write down every detail, to share exactly how it all happened. Every conversation I remember having with anyone who influenced our love will be recalled, for this is our story…

It was a beautiful Tuesday in the third week of March, 1956. My nursery was starting to boom with flowers. In just a few years' time, it had become the most well-known garden and nursery in Baghdad, and royalty and elite persons visited from all over. I was on the roof of my house, talking to Mr. Radhi about how I wanted my new house to be, my beautiful place facing the Tigris, when I noticed a blonde lady and two other people entering from the front. I didn't have a clear view of them, but what I saw was enough for me to consider greeting them personally right away.

The young lady, whom I assumed was British, looked to be in her early twenties, and she was the most attractive woman I'd ever seen. She was so exquisite that all the colorful flowers around her seemed to fade. She was stunning, rather tall, with a perfect figure. Her long, golden hair shone like sunlight breaking through the clouds, and her big, sparkling eyes were greener than any leaves or grass I'd seen. Her eyebrows were so perfect that they looked as if they'd been drawn by hand, and her cheeks were rosy enough to make my roses shy away. Her lips were naturally full and colorful. She was wearing a long white dress with a green ribbon in the middle, fastened with a golden brooch. I wished life would stand still in that moment, just so I could have had an eternity to absorb the beauty of that masterpiece of creation in front of me. My heart was beating so fast, and I was totally swept away. I had never felt like that before, as if I'd been somehow transported to a place I'd never thought existed. After I got my sanity back, thanks to a few deep breaths, I introduced myself and Mr. Radhi, who had joined me after I suddenly took off and left him stranded on the rooftop.

The lady was shy and didn't answer, but the older Iraqi woman next to her spoke in a low, clear voice. She was in her sixties, a bit short, with small, dark brown eyes. Her face was covered in wrinkles, and her hair was gray. Still, there was a warm feeling about her. She was sweet enough to compliment the place and said she'd heard a lot about it. She got straight to the point about their visit and told me they wanted a nice bouquet of flowers to give to a general. "Mary's father has been gone for months, training with the Royal Guard, and we want to give him something beautiful," she said.

As soon as I heard Mary's name, it seemed to ring in my ears, even as I looked at their traveling companion, an older man. Like Mary, he didn't speak a word. He was a typical Englishman, like those I'd seen several times in Baghdad, but he was very tall. He seemed to be in his sixties and was wearing a British hat, holding a cane in his right hand. I assumed he was the butler or some sort of house security. I politely asked them to have a seat near the fountain and enjoy some tea until we could prepare their wonderful bouquet.

I tried to catch as many glimpses of Mary as I could without being too conspicuous. She never dared to look back to me. Mr. Radhi noticed that I was looking at her, and he gave me a strict stare—a look I hadn't seen from him before. When the bouquet was ready and they finished their tea, the old lady paid, the Englishman finally spoke to thank us, and they left.

After they were gone, Mr. Radhi gave me that same disapproving look again.

I shrugged. "Only a blind man wouldn't have wanted to look at her," I told him.

"Well, in that case, you'd better be blind next time," he replied.

"You really think there will be a next time?" I asked.

"Son, this is no joke. I am dead serious, Ali," Mr. Radhi said loudly. "You must be careful of—"

I interrupted, "It's not only her looks. It's everything about her. I-I can't explain it. I just felt something when I saw her. Something inside me wouldn't let me take my eyes off her. I don't know how to explain it, but there was some sort of connection—if not a physical one, something spiritual—some power pushing me toward her. And Mr. Radhi, before you answer or lecture me about acting childish, I have to say this wasn't normal. I know I don't know her, but I immediately felt something deep for her, just from that one look."

"Ali, I am going to say this once, and I won't repeat it again. No matter what you decide, you know I will be on your side and will support you. But there are borders in life, Ali. No matter the temptation, no matter how right and wonderful it might seem to cross those borders, they should never be crossed. This Mary, my son, is a red line, a border you should not ignore." He looked at me with a serious expression on his face, one of sternness and compassion. "From the time you came into our lives, I have gotten to know you. That's what scares me, Ali. You are a stubborn, very determined person, and while this has helped you achieve your dreams in business, it might also lead you into bigger conflicts from all sides. You and this Mary are from entirely different worlds, something you are too young to understand and powerless to face. Life isn't fair, Ali. As much as we want it to, equality has never and never will exist. If you go forward with pursuing this girl, the path will be hard for you. They are foreigners, and they will not be here forever. They know nothing of our daily lives. We are not the same. Someday, if things get serious on the political or social front, you might see what I mean. Maybe then the blinkers will come off and you will see the true colors of the world. Deep down inside, we don't look at each other the same way. We differ in culture, social habits, beliefs, and, most importantly, politics. Her father is a general, Ali. You cannot go after a Royal Guard general's daughter and expect your people to support you." With that, Mr. Radhi took off, but it was a conversation I would not soon forget.

True to his word, he never brought the issue up again, and he supported me in whatever decisions I made. He was there for me every step of the way, as I imagine my father would have done if he had lived. Mr. Radhi had a special place in my heart, because I knew he did more for me than any man ever would, simply out of the kindness of his heart.

As the days passed, I tried to immerse myself in my work and the remodeling of my home. Still, despite the reality of every word Mr. Radhi had spoken, I remained under Mary's unspoken spell. She was constantly on my mind, day and night. I ached for her, and Mr. Radhi and Madam Laila's absence didn't help to ease my loneliness. At that time of year, they always traveled to London for a month, to spend time at a nice estate they owned. They had asked me to join them several times, but I'd always been too busy. This time, though, I wished I'd gone with them, just to get away from my work and my obsessive thoughts of Mary for a while.

Whenever I heard anyone arriving at our place, I'd rush down to meet them, hoping to see her. I kept my eye on the gate constantly, and if I had to leave for any reason, I told my helpers to come find me as soon as possible if the beautiful blonde, green-eyed British lady showed up. I claimed she was an important buyer I needed to handle personally.

It wouldn't have been impossible to find her on my own, but I didn't want to. I knew she'd return sooner or later, and that would give me a better chance to take the next step. The last thing I wanted to do was force myself on her or scare her away.

As the weeks passed, there was obvious change in me, evident to everyone who knew me. I was eating less, I wasn't that cheerful, and my ever-present joy had faded. Only Mr. Radhi knew the reason behind it, but out of respect, he didn't tell a soul—not even his wife, Madam Laila, who'd also noticed the change after their return to Iraq. She never asked me about it and gave me my space.

When Mustafa came back from one of his trips, he knew something was wrong with me, and he instantly wanted answers. He asked for some tea and pulled me over beside the fountain. Like some kind of scavenger on a corpse, he was all over me, demanding that I tell him what was going on. He was very worried, and it was useless trying to keep a secret from him; one way or another, he'd eventually get it out of me.

I told him the whole story, and his reaction was similar to Mr. Radhi's. He told me I was getting myself into trouble and continued to lecture me and give me his harsh opinions. He told me stories of women he'd had emotional feelings for during his travels, women he decided not to pursue because it was too much of a headache. "And my circumstances are nothing compared to yours! Why, once I met this woman in India who—"

He was in the middle of one of his love stories when Mary and the old lady came inside. I jumped out of my seat, left Mustafa in a fraction of a second, and hurried to greet them. In spite of losing my parents at a young age, I'd always believed I was a lucky person, and everything had surprisingly fallen into place for me. This was yet another example, for they wanted me to get a look at their garden, which needed some loving care and a whole lot of change and updating. In my head, I was dancing with joy. I knew that was my chance, and I couldn't have wished for a better platform. I had to make it wonderful not only because I loved my work, but also because in the end, that garden would be hers.

We decided on a date, and my name would be left with security so I'd have no trouble entering. Up to that point, Mary didn't say a word; all talking was done by the old lady, Miss Naseema, who'd become well known to me by then. Just as they were about to leave, Mary, careful to avoid eye contact, said, "Thank you," very quietly. Her words were as soft as she was, and from the moment they entered my ears, her sweet and tender voice became part of my soul.

I went back to Mustafa, who'd seen the whole thing, but before I could excitedly tell him that she was the woman I'd been talking about, he warned, "Ali, it's wrong, I have a bad feeling about this. I can't blame you for falling for a creature so beautiful, but believe me, dear cousin, I sense trouble. You shouldn't let things go any farther, Ali. We are simple people, and we live easy lives. Why complicate things? I'm happy you are doing well. Don't throw this opportunity away over the love of a woman who isn't right for you."

"Mustafa, we have the right to love, don't we? I'm human, and I have feelings and emotions. Just give me a chance to prove to you that this can work out. Of course I won't force the lady into anything. I have to try because in my gut, I know there is something serious about the way I feel for her. I know you think I'm crazy, cousin, but I promise you, Mustafa, that this beautiful young lady will be my wife sometime. I promise you that," I replied back.

Mustafa had known me since childhood, and he knew how stubborn I could be. Realizing there was nothing he could say to talk me out of it, he just patted me on the back and left.

* * *

My meeting was scheduled for a Tuesday, and I dressed very professionally in a navy-blue suit and a red tie, along with a matching red rose. At the security gate outside the compound, I was asked several routine questions for the sake of identification, and once they'd confirmed my name and all the information, they allowed me inside.

The house was located in an extremely secure special compound in Baghdad, were many foreigners resided. Few Iraqis were allowed to entry, and only by invitation. It looked nothing like any part of Baghdad I'd ever seen. It was very quiet, the streets were paved differently, and everything was very organized and clean. Children were playing in one of the small parks. There were basketball and volleyball courts, a soccer field, and a big swimming pool shared by everyone in the compound. People of different ages were bicycling, and others were walking their dogs. If someone had been taken there in a blindfold, they wouldn't have known they were still in Baghdad, because everything about the place and the culture inside it was entirely different. All the houses were similar: three-story villas, off-white in color, with long, marble garages. The only thing that differentiated one from another were the small alterations each family added to their domiciles, like the decorations on the outside doors or walls and adornments in some of the outdoor gardens.

I was welcomed inside by Mr. Dalton, the man who'd accompanied them the first time they'd come to visit our nursery. He'd been working for the family for over eighteen years, and he was now in charge of the household, though his responsibilities differed greatly from those of the butler's.

We sat down on the terrace that overlooked the garden, which was comprised of a nice but simple, fairly green lawn speckled with a few random flowers here and there. After we had tea and made small talk about my life, Mr. Dalton gave me a tour of the garden. I heard every word he said as we walked, but my mind was elsewhere, focused solely on Mary. I wondered where she was and if I was going to see her or not. I didn't want to ask Mr. Dalton or the owners about her, because it would have seemed inappropriate. They had invited me there to do a job, and I didn't want to seem too forward.

The garden stretched all around the house. It was largest in the front and was connected to the back garden by a very narrow strip of lawn that had nothing planted in it. The back garden was a bit smaller in size and wasn't in good shape. The grass was awfully overgrown, as if it hadn't been mown in weeks, and there were yellow patches everywhere. Truly, their gardens needed my help.

There were two balconies on the second floor overlooking the back garden, and when Mr. Dalton saw me looking at them, he informed me that those were the upper bedrooms, one for the general and the other for his daughter. He then informed me that the main reason they wanted the gardens renovated was to satisfy the wishes of Mary, the general's daughter. As Mr. Dalton explained it to me, she'd just come back from the UK, where she'd been studying poetry for three years. He told me she had lived in Baghdad for a year and a half before, when her father's military service transferred him there from Cairo some five years earlier. I was glad to learn more about Mary from Mr. Dalton, but most of all, I was anxious to see her.

I was already explaining to Mr. Dalton what I had in mind for the front and back gardens when Mary and Miss Naseema headed our way. Mary looked like the purest rose I'd ever seen in her pale pink dress with the matching parasol. As they greeted me, I caught the sparkle in her eye and shyly told them hello.

Mr. Dalton explained to them what he'd told me about the garden, and then Miss Naseema took over. "We trust you to choose the right look for our gardens, Ali," she said. "We'd love to see more color out here, especially reds and yellows, which are the general's favorite. We need more trees and flowers to be planted, a landscape design that will brighten up this part of the dull compound. We've almost accidentally entered our neighbor's house so many times because everything looks so identical! If it wasn't for their dog, I would have just barged right in!" she joked. "We want our gardens to be something special, a unique design, and Mary is sure you're the right man for the job."

As she spoke, I took plenty of notes and asked questions so I could get it just right.

Mary said nothing until Miss Naseema began to talk about the back yard. At that point, the beautiful young woman chimed in, "Mr. Ali, I am quite confident in your abilities, as I've seen your wonderful work. I'm sure everything will look lovely and inviting in the end. I have two personal requests for this side of the garden. My room is on the right up there. Every morning, I have breakfast on the balcony, and I'd love to have something beautiful to look at while I sip my tea. I am very fond of orchids, so please plant as many as you can. Secondly, would it be possible to plant strawberries? I'd love to pick them when they're red, ripe, and juicy."

My heart trembled with every word she said. I'd shown up expecting little more than a glance from her or possibly a "Good morning" or a "Thank you,' but now she was talking to me, going on and on about the garden of her dreams. Her words were music to my ears, like a beautiful poem or a melody so sweet that I never wanted it to end. I couldn't believe she'd actually addressed me by name, and I was flattered by her confidence in me being able to grant her requests to beautify the grounds she gazed upon every morning.

I tried to act normal and to keep my voice from quivering as I replied, "Miss Mary, you needn't be so formal. Please call me only Ali. I'd like to thank you for the kind words about my work and for having faith in me. It really means a lot to me that you admire my work. Rest assured that you will have all the orchids and strawberries your heart desires. I will personally make sure of it and will do all I can to make this garden mirror the beauty of the one who looks upon it over her teacup each morning."

She gave me a slight smile and shied away a bit as she replied, "Thanks, Ali. And please call me only Mary."

We all agreed that I would start the work in a fortnight, as I had previous engagements and obligations to tend to. I took off my hat out of respect and bid them farewell.

On the way back, I was ecstatic, happier than I'd ever been before. I felt I was flying, as if my steps were bouncing on a cloud. I couldn't get her smile out of my mind, and I remembered every word her lovely lips had uttered. The way she'd said my name went through my mind time and time again and kept ringing in my ears.

To calm myself down a bit, I took a seat on the pavement, not even worrying about the soiling or wrinkling it might cause to my suit. I tried to think the whole thing over logically, without letting my heart or its yearnings get in the way. It was difficult to grasp what was really going on, but I had a certain sense that there was something brewing between us. I said aloud, "I think she likes me. No, I *know* she does! Yes, Mary likes me," I said, as if trying to reassure myself, my voice getting louder with every word. I was confident that there was a special bond connecting us, and I was sure it was more of a reality than just my dream. I felt our union was our destiny, that we were meant to be together. By the time I got up from the pavement, an ear-to-ear smile had stretched across my face. *Only two weeks from now, I'll see her again,* I thought and grinned even wider.

In the days that followed, I stayed busy with my house. The rebuild was going as planned, and within five or six months, I hoped to have a beautiful house on the river, just behind my nursery, a house that would be any man's dream. It would be two levels, with three bedrooms, a dining room, a living room, a big kitchen, and a beautiful terrace that led to a backyard garden next to the river. The house would have a separate entrance from the nursery so that when work was over, I could rest in a world all my own.

Madam Laila came several times with some delicious food for me and the gentlemen working there. She also wanted to make sure I was all right and asked if I needed anything. I told her everything I was feeling inside because I couldn't hide it any longer; after all, she was like a mother to me. I knew she saw the sincerity in my eyes when I spoke of Mary.

When I was finished talking, she hugged me and said some beautiful words I will never forget: "As much as I agree with all those who have advised you before that this might be a mistake, something too risky and complicated, I see the happiness dancing in your eyes whenever you mention her, Ali. I know a feeling like that only comes once in a lifetime, and I think you should follow your heart's desires. I believe in love, and I know love conquers all." She was sincerely happy for me, and she'd often hinted that I should find someone to start a family with, so she couldn't hide her joy when I told her about Mary.

⁘

I carefully planned out the renovation of Mary's gardens and gathered all the various seeds, making sure not to forget her strawberries. I couldn't wait to plant them for her, and I hoped the bright, red fruit would make her happy and remind her of me.

When the long-awaited time of the renovation finally came, I took Hassan with me, a young gardener who'd been working with me from the start. Hassan was smart and always knew exactly what I wanted by just looking at the plans I drew up; I had made sure he knew how to read and write and spent an hour teaching him every day after work. This time, as with all of our previous assignments, I laid out the plan and advised him on some issues about the final design of the gardens. Usually, I would have left all the work to him and only returned in the end to make sure it had been properly executed, but I wanted to be directly involved with Mary's project. Besides, I thought that would afford me more opportunities to see her, so I decided that Hassan and I would take turns, each one of us showing up once a week.

It was a beautiful day, and we arrived early in the morning. Mr. Dalton showed us in and offered us breakfast, which we politely declined since we'd already eaten and were anxious to get to work. After thanking him, we excused ourselves so we could go out and get things underway. I showed Hassan the young lady's

53

balcony and indicated where we needed to plant the orchids she had requested. I also outlined the area where the strawberries would go. I wanted to make sure he understood everything perfectly: where the roses, orchids, and gardenias would be placed; what tulips were to be planted; and which colors of each plant were to be used in each location. I then focused on the ficus trees for their outdoor entrance; this was important because it was the starting point of the garden, the place where people would catch their first glimpse of the beauty of our work. Hassan had a natural gift in perfectly placing and designing ficus tree layouts, and the whole front area would be bordered with them, with a bigger one at the end, forming almost a conical shape.

After twenty minutes of planning, we agreed on everything and were ready to get started, since we had little time to waste. As soon as Hassan was finished with the mowing, he would plant roses and seeds in the front, while I was working on the back yard.

As always, I started by outlining the garden. I dug a third foot all around the area and filled it with smashed silver and dark maroon pebbles, colors I felt were a good match for the area. As I toiled away, I continuously looked up at Mary's room, hoping she'd open the door and come to the balcony, fantasizing about how gorgeous she would look standing up there above me, like an angel of the morning. Whenever I thought I heard a noise, my heart started beating faster. I couldn't wait to see her, but hours passed, and no one came.

Way past noon when Mr. Dalton came out again and asked what time we could take a break so lunch could be served. Like the chatterbox he always was, Mr. Dalton informed me that Mary and Miss Naseema, had traveled to the UK with the general few days earlier.

*What?! She's gone back to England?* It was shocking, bad news to me, and it felt as if someone had shot me in the back with a sharp arrow. My whole world seemed to turn black and crumble around me, and I couldn't see a thing. I tried to hide the disappointment, but I was hopelessly desperate to see her, and it showed in my face. When Mr. Dalton asked what was wrong, I had to make up an excuse about some sudden pain in my back from my work, and I told him I hadn't slept well the night before.

When he continued talking, I realized the news wasn't that bad; I was quite relieved to learn that they'd be back, but I was still disappointed. I'd had high hopes of seeing her during the work, but those hopes were dashed. I began doubting that I'd ever have a chance to get to know her, and questions poured through my mind: *What if she never comes back? Have I just been imagining that there is a connection between us? Has this all been in my head like some romantic fairytale? Maybe something important, something urgent happened in the UK and they had to go.* I was anxious to know more, and I couldn't stand being left without the details and the answers to all the questions. I asked Mr. Dalton, "How long will they be gone, and do they leave Baghdad often?"

Mr. Dalton was kind enough to tell me that they visited the UK at that time of year every year to commemorate the anniversary of her mother's passing at an annual family gathering. "They'll be there for several weeks to be with family and pay their respects, but then they'll be back," he assured me. After he answered my questions, he began talking about Miss Naseema. "Mary's real mother passed away when Mary was only six, but Miss Naseema has been like a mother to the girl for over fifteen years, ever since the general was appointed in Cairo." Mr. Dalton then explained that because the general's work kept him very busy and often required that he be away from the house, Miss Naseema and Mr. Dalton himself were the closest to Mary.

As I listened to Mr. Dalton's words, I began to feel even closer to Mary. Like me, she was somewhat of an orphan; we had even more in common than I had imagined.

After our little talk ended, I called Hassan so we could have lunch together, and then we finished our day's work before the Maghrib prayer and left.

Over the course of the next two weeks, I passed by several times, and lunch with Mr. Dalton was always interesting and very informative, much to my delight.

✺

It was a normal day at our nursery, and I hadn't passed by the general's home in just over a week. Much to my surprise, I was visited by Mr. Dalton, who came to inform me that the general, Mary, and Miss Naseema had returned.

"The general would like to see you tomorrow afternoon over tea so he can personally thank you for the work done on his glorious garden," he said,

The news couldn't have been better. I was glad she was back at last, and I was sure she'd love the changes we'd made to the garden. Despite the fact that it would take several more weeks for the flowers to blossom and the strawberries to be ready for picking, the grounds still looked amazing. I could only sleep for a couple hours that night, for I was literally counting down the minutes until I'd be able to see her again.

When I arrived the next day to meet with the general, I saw that Hassan had done a great job over the past week. Everything was in place, and every inch of the garden was immaculately mown and trimmed. The layout was beautiful, perhaps one of our best jobs yet.

The general was nothing like I'd imagined him to be. He politely and casually introduced himself and welcomed me in. After he thanked me for my work, he asked me to sit down for some tea and biscuits. He was a man of average build and medium height, just a little chubby. His hair was entirely gray, and his matching eyebrows were thick and knitted slightly together over the bridge of his nose. He looked older than he was, and it was instantly obvious that Mary had inherited her good looks from her late mother, though she did have her father's striking green eyes.

He was accompanied by a well-built, young, blond man with a square jaw, dark brown eyes, and a sharp nose. The bodyguard was in his early thirties and looked to be the general's right arm. He was a cocky, arrogant lieutenant, and when I offered to shake his hand, he just greeted me without taking it. My first impression about him that he was a bitter man, a man filled with hate, and little did I know how right I was.

After we enjoyed our tea and biscuits, I thanked him for his hospitality and offered to give a garden tour to the gentlemen so I could explain what we had done. I assured the general that in a month's time, the flowers would decorate the place in a rainbow of colors and that his garden would be so lovely that he wouldn't want to leave it.

The general was clearly very happy with our work, but the snobbish young lieutenant wasn't really satisfied. Every time I spoke, he uttered complaints and tried to belittle what we'd done and make a mockery of the information I was giving them. "Flowers are flowers," he said. "All you have to do is give them water and watch them bloom for a day, and then they eventually rot," he complained, then chuckled at his own cruel words. After only ten minutes of going around the garden, he informed the general, "Sir, we've wasted quite a bit of time out here." Then he turned to me and said, "We have some real work and business to attend to now, if you don't mind."

The general didn't apologize for his rude bodyguard, but he cleared his throat and politely thanked me again, and they excused themselves and left.

I had a few things to do in the garden, so I walked toward the back yard.

"Ali, it's wonderful! I'm coming down!" I heard a melodious voice call from the balcony.

I was overwhelmed at the sight of Mary, and while it only took her a minute to come down, but it felt like hours to my poor, rapidly beating heart. My emotions got the better of me as soon as I saw her, and without thinking, I blurted out. "I missed you, Mary." When I saw how taken aback and surprised she was by my forwardness, I quickly tried to correct my mistake. "Um, I mean…I wish you had been here to see the garden come together day by day. I would have loved to see your reaction, especially when we planted the orchids and strawberries."

She smiled again and replied, "I would have loved to have seen that, but I had to be with my family. I hope everyone was helpful."

"Yes, and Mr. Dalton is especially kind and friendly. I hope you're satisfied with what we've done here."

"Oh very! I'm so happy that I can look out here and enjoy the view. I always thought it was a pity that this garden was never used properly all those years, but thanks to you, that has changed."

"I gave the general and the gentleman with him a short tour," I told her.

"That was very kind of you, Ali…and it's even more kind that you refer to Charles as a gentleman. That's more than he deserves. There's nothing gentle about him, believe me," she said, wincing as she thought of him.

59

"I don't want to be judgmental, but I had a feeling about him. I don't think anything pleases him," I quickly responded.

Mary laughed. "Can you believe my father wants me to marry him? I wouldn't consider him if he was the last man on Earth. Besides, I don't want to marry a military man. I barely know my father because he's a general, and I won't subject myself to that in a husband."

Not wanting to give away how elated I was about her saying that, I just nodded. I was glad to know that she had no interest in Charles, but I also realized he might be trouble. If I wanted to have a relationship with Mary, I would have to be very careful.

As I continued showing her around, she listened to every word I said about the garden. I explained in detail the best time for trimming the trees, when the grass should be watered, and when the flowers could be picked for beautiful centerpiece bouquets. After I finished telling her all about the garden, I felt it was time to leave. I bid her goodbye and told her if she ever needed anything, she was welcome to stop by my place. On my way out, I looked at a beautiful red rose and was about to cut it, but then I turned to Mary. "This is your garden, so perhaps I should ask your permission before I cut this rose?"

She nodded.

I cut the flower gently from its stem and gave it to her.

When our hands touched a bit as she took it, she blushed.

"I couldn't see this beautiful rose anywhere but in your hands. Have a nice day, Mary," I said softly as I made my way out.

I was still in my car when Miss Naseema, who'd seemingly seen Mary and I together, approached and called me by my name. "Ali, can I talk to you?" Before I could even reply, she'd already gotten into my car. "I know you're an honorable man, but don't forget who she is and who her father is. You're an Iraqi, and they will never let the two of you be together. You should put this out of your mind and forget about it, or it will just be more painful for everyone in the long run." With that, she opened my car door and got out and walked back into the house.

I was completely shocked. Everything had gone so well until she got into my car and ruined my day with her warnings, the same one so many others had given me. As wonderful as it had been to talk and walk with Mary, I was still Iraqi, and she was still a British general's daughter, so I was faced with the same dilemma.

I tried to weigh my options and digest my feelings bit by bit. Mary and I were from entirely different worlds, cultures, and status. Even the simplest of things would be complicated for us. I wouldn't be able to get into the compound without an invitation. In that way, even in my own country, I was an outsider. Furthermore, I couldn't even imagine what a scandal and rumor mill such a relationship would cause in the community. On the other hand, I already deeply loved Mary, and I knew I had to overcome all obstacles to have her in my life.

When I finally arrived back at my place, I just stared at the half-finished home. In a few months, it would be complete, the most beautiful home I could possibly imagine, but it would be far too empty without the right person to share it with. I knew that person Was Mary. She was my destiny. I knew that with all my heart, and I could just feel it, even if everything and everyone around us seemed to be against us.

In spite of the storm in my mind and heart, the weather was wonderful that day, so I headed to the dock area near the river, eager to take a ride on my little wooden motorboat. I hoped it would help me clear my head. The river flowed steadily, and with every passing minute, I felt more relaxed on that calm, rippling water, cooled by the comfortable, fresh air.

I passed by some small fishing boats, and the old fishermen waved to me above their stretched nets as I greeted them. It was the time of day when they had to clean their nets so they could lay them out for the next day's catch. One of the fishermen even pointed to me and asked me to join him. *Why not?* I thought to myself, so I moved closer to his boat so I could hear what he had to say.

"Do you like fish?" he asked in a gruff voice.

"I certainly do," I answered.

He took one out of a small, oval-shaped bowl. "This is my best catch of the morning," he said, holding it up for me to look at. "You're lucky, I guess, because I somehow left it behind when I took the fish to market.

You seem like a nice enough boy. Why don't you take it?" the fisherman offered.

"Thank you," I said and took the fish from him.

"How about some tea?" he asked.

Tea sounded wonderful, so I was happy to join him for a cup. We each stood on our respective boats, talking, sipping, and watching the sun go down. It is said that with age comes wisdom, and after that day and speaking with that man, I knew that to be true.

The old river fisherman was in his late sixties, and he could tell by looking at me that I had a lot on my mind. He wasn't the least bit shy and immediately asked, "What's bothering you most right now, at this moment?"

I did need someone to talk to, and I didn't see anything wrong with opening up to that kind, wise old soul right there in the river. "I-I'm lost," I stuttered. "I have a choice to make, and I'm not sure which path to take."

The old fisherman's answer was one I would not soon forget: "My son, it's not about what direction you should take. It's about choosing one direction and working to move forward on that path, no matter what. Think of this boat. If I don't control it and leave it to float by itself, the waves or tides will always control my path and take me wherever they please, whether I like it or not. If I decide to take a certain path, be it easy or difficult, and no matter how strong the tide is and what lies ahead, I can choose to steer my boat. I don't have regrets or doubts in my life because I always choose what I want to do. No matter what I have to face and how challenging it is, I have the comfort of knowing that all things are consequences of my own choices, and I am happy to have the chance to choose. Do not wait for the tide to take you, my boy. Instead, you take on the tide"

After Haji Ibrahim spoke those words, all of my doubts melted away. *No matter what lies ahead,* I told myself, *I will be happy with the choice I made, and I will do whatever it takes to keep moving forward on that path.* At long last, I felt happy and relieved, and with the old man's words repeating in my mind, I turned the boat around and bid my new friend farewell. My choice was made: I wanted Mary, and I would have her, even if it meant fighting against the whole world.

# Chapter 3

The Fajir prayer was called just before dawn. It was the first of five prayers required by each Muslim every day, and all prayers had to be prayed at a specific time. Adnan couldn't believe he'd spent over seven hours reading. He yawned, stretched, and set the book aside, then left his shop, locked it behind him, and walked to the nearest mosque.

The mosque was nearly empty, and only a dozen or so people were there to pray, most of them local elderly folks. Ever since the end of the war, people had avoided the Fajir prayer for security reasons, but those who'd suffered hard lives couldn't have cared less and insisted on following their religious customs in spite of all the turmoil and hardship.

After finishing his prayers, Adnan decided to take a short walk. The quietness of the streets gave Adnan some time to think properly. He was still very confused about how the book about the gardener had ended up in his bookshop in the first place. He wondered who had put it there. He was eager to continue reading, but his body had already shut down. He felt drained, and he knew he had to get a few hours' sleep, especially since he had to open his shop at nine a.m., so he went back to the shop to rest.

Four and half hours later, he opened the shop. It was just before nine, and those few hours of sleep had really helped to rejuvenate Adnan. Aside from a kink in his neck, he felt fresh and awake. He decided it was best to focus on his work and continue reading the mysterious book after lunchtime.

His wife stopped by at nine thirty with some breakfast. She'd missed him and had been worried about him all night. Adnan told her about the book he'd found and how addictive and interesting the story was. She seemed intrigued, but she said, "Adnan, why don't you just come home early and bring the book with you to read it there? It's too dangerous to stay overnight here."

They enjoyed breakfast and went on talking about the house and the kids. Just before she left, he promised to be home later that night.

Samir, a man who wanted to buy the shop from Adnan, dropped by the shop just before lunch. Samir was an avid reader and had been a customer for years.

Adnan offered him some tea, and they sat down to talk about the store. Adnan was still not convinced of selling it, and finding that book yesterday hadn't made the decision any easier. He already felt as if he was sitting on a vast sea of knowledge, and he thought that finding that unique handwritten book inside another book's cover was a sign that he shouldn't go on with the sale. The owner and potential buyer went in circles and could come to no solid agreement. Finally, Adnan admitted, "I appreciate you stopping by, Samir, but I'm afraid I'm just not ready to make a decision yet. I need more time."

After Samir left, Adnan had lunch with some friends at a nearby restaurant, a place where he'd been enjoying good meals and company for the past three decades. He always had the quzi, tasty rice with a big chunk of meat; unlike Iraq's political situation over the years, that dish hadn't changed a bit and was still just as delicious as ever. During lunch, he asked his friends, "Do you know of anyone who has had a business in this area for a long time? Anyone who might remember a lot of people and events from the past?"

"Well," one of Adnan's friends chimed in, "my uncle is eighty, and he remembers everything about Baghdad. He's also good with names. He can even tell you which minister was in charge of which ministry in each year. He remembers the goal-scorers from football matches played decades ago, and if you get him started talking about his childhood, he'll never stop."

Adnan was happy to hear it, and he hoped the old man might be able to give him some insights into Ali's story. "Do you think I could talk to your uncle? Maybe tomorrow afternoon?" Adnan asked, not wanting to give too much away. He figured that would give him enough time to finish the book, and if what Ali had written was true, the old man might have some knowledge about it.

"Sure," his friend said. "I'll arrange for him to meet you at the café a block away, where all those old fellows gather to play dominos and backgammon. My uncle has a memory as sharp as a tack, and he's also friendly and funny and loves to talk. I think you'll like him, Adnan, and I know he'll like you."

After Adnan finished his lunch and returned to his shop, the remainder of the day was quiet and uneventful. Before he knew it, it was already six in the evening. He closed the shop and called his wife to tell her he was going to stay overnight again. He knew he was breaking a promise and that she'd be upset with him, but he had to finish the book before meeting with his friend's uncle, and being at home would be too distracting. He needed a quiet place, a place where he could be all alone and not bothered by any noise.

After he hung up with his disgruntled wife, he took out his small black notebook in which he'd written down some important facts from the book he'd been reading. He set the notebook aside and opened Ali's memoir to continue where he'd left off the night before, about halfway through the book...

༚༝༚

The fisherman's words affected me greatly, and I decided to take action, but I had to be slow and cautious about it, so as not to arouse suspicions. Miss Naseema's advice was important. I knew I'd have to carefully study every step I made, and every piece would have to fall in place at the right time. I couldn't take any chances because this wasn't just a joke or some teenage crush. My love and desire for Mary were very real, but so were the dangers of pursuing her. Charles, the general's ever-present sidekick, was one of those dangers, a determined man of a seemingly evil nature; everything about him felt wrong, so I would have to exercise precautions in all dealings with him and those who spoke to him. Most of all, I had to be sure of Mary's feelings. I didn't want to surprise or frighten her, and I knew I couldn't force her to love me. I had to be certain that she shared my affection, and I had to make sure she knew what our togetherness would cost. A relationship between us would inevitably change both of our lives dramatically and forever.

I knew I had to remain focused on my ultimate goal, being with Mary, if everything was going to fall into place. I had to finish my work on the general's gardens and make them as beautiful as possible, I had to maintain my successful gardening business, and I needed to finish my dream home; the latter was the best excuse to continue seeking what my heart so longed for, Mary.

The memories of Mr. Radhi's first house party still lingered in my mind. I wanted to host a gathering like that, to invite the important people I knew. My guest list would include my loyal customers, and of course the general's family would top it. On that happy occasion, I would finally approach Mary with my feelings.

Until that day came, I still wanted to see her as much as possible. I started making sporadic visits to Mary's house, using the excuse that I wanted to check on the garden. I wanted to stay in the picture, to make her feel, one way or another, that I was always close by, always available to her. I hoped she would gradually come to understand how genuinely interested I was so that when the right moment came, she wouldn't be surprised or frightened about my affection for her.

I executed my plan to the last detail. I visited them every two to three weeks to make sure everything was all right. During those visits, I always spoke with Mary or Mr. Dalton about the garden. It seemed to bring joy to Mary's eyes when I visited, and whenever I was alone with her even for a few seconds, I made sure to compliment her; that always put a smile on her face, and I loved to make her happy.

With Miss Naseema ever by her side, Mary visited me several times. On one of those visits, I told her about the party I was going to have. "It's in two weeks," I said, "and of course you and everyone in your household are invited."

Mary couldn't hide her beautiful, gleaming smile and was glad to accept the invitation on behalf of them all.

Just when she was about to leave, when Miss Naseema quite a ways ahead and already near their car, I moved closer to Mary and had the courage to whisper some words in her ear: "Mary, the party I'm throwing is for you. I want to...I have something to share with you."

She responded with a slight nod, her eyes full of anticipation.

✦✦✦

Within a few days, my friends and assistants had delivered the invitations, a simple but beautiful note card with a rose attached to the side. The party would be on September 7, the historic day when I would profess my undying love to Mary. It had only been six months since I'd first laid eyes on her, but it felt like we'd known each other for years. I hoped that in a matter of days, she'd tell me she felt the same way.

Mustafa returned to Baghdad for the party. I'd informed him of it a month earlier, and there was no way in the world he would miss it. I'd already spoken to him about my decision to talk to Mary. He was tired of trying to talk me out of it, so, like the close cousin and friend he was, he finally gave up and decided to help me. Just his support and advice boosted my confidence; Mustafa had learned quite a bit out in the world and from his own romantic encounters and experiences, and he was happy to tell me all he knew.

Madam Laila was thrilled with my new home and was more than happy to take charge of the preparations. She made arrangements for catering and organized the whole thing. She was quite an expert in event planning, and she knew exactly what we would need to create a wonderful evening for everyone in attendance. If I'd ever known anyone classy, Madam Laila was certainly that, so I was happy to put her in charge of my party and grateful for all her hard work, insights, and help.

I loved music, so to make the evening even more special, I asked some friends to install speakers around the garden so my guests could enjoy classical music in the background as they arrived. One of my clients had given me two classical music record albums, and I had immediately fallen in love with Mozart and Johan Strauss. Strauss's "Voices of Spring" was my absolute favorite and had to be played.

The night before the party seemed to drag on and on. I barely slept because I was so excited about the next day. I had it all planned out in my head, but the execution of that plan was only a day away, and I was a bit apprehensive about it. I worried that others may have been right and that I should have kept my distance from Mary. *What if she does see me as just the gardener, someone lowly and not worthy of a relationship with her? Even if she does have feelings for me, what if she's decided it's too impossibly difficult for us to be together? What if she thinks the barriers that differ and separate us are not able to be conquered, and she's decided to rely on logic rather than her feelings?* I thought and pondered and worried all night, but in the end, no matter the outcome, my mind was set. *I will tell Mary how I feel. She must know.*

All I had to do was to choose the right moment to take her away from the crowd and talk to her in private. I knew the party would be my best opportunity for that, and there would be no better circumstances. *It could be my last chance,* I thought, *and I have to prove myself worthy of her.* Mary had to know that what I felt inside for her was true and real, that the burning love I had for her had to come out. She had to be certain of my true intentions. I didn't want to mask my desires. I wanted to be an open book, to be myself and let her know that my intentions were sincere. Simply put, I wanted Mary to know I loved her—that I loved her more than anything or anyone in the world.

‛⁄‛

There were around 140 invited guests, and only 35 were non-Iraqis, 2 English families who were close friends of Mr. Radhi and Madam Laila's, and some of my clients like the ambassador of India, a family from France, an American family, and the Thompsons, Mary's Family. I was sure that dreadful Charles would accompany them, of course, because he always followed the general around like some lost puppy. My Iraqi guests were a mixture of friends and clients, including some important physicians, journalists, wealthy businessman, and Dr. Kamal Adel, a cardiologist who had studied in Moscow and would later play a very important role in my life. My uncle and my cousin, Mustafa, also attended.

The party was set up in my back yard, right next to the river. My uncle, myself, Mr. Radhi, and Madam Laila greeted the guests, who all started to arrive just before noon. The place looked fantastic. All the chairs and tables were delicately covered with white and gold cloth, the eating utensils were perfectly polished, and there was a big bouquet of flowers on each table, each one carefully selected by me. The classical music in the background made for a festive atmosphere, and thanks mostly to Madam Laila, my home looked like a royal palace.

Although I had a smile on my face while greeting every guest, I was anxiously waiting for only one—my future, my motivation, and my only desire in the world. Finally after half of the other guests arrived, the Thompsons showed up. I wasn't sure a living creature in our world or any other had ever been more beautiful than my Mary. Her hair was brushed to the side, covering nearly half of her soft face. Her green eyes sparkled like precious emeralds. She was an angel sent to Earth, an angel in a white and red dress fit for a princess, and she was right there, at my party. My heart skipped several beats, and the second I shook her dainty hand and we exchanged looks for a fraction of a second, it felt as if my heart had stopped altogether. As soon as Mary and her family walked past us, Madam Laila smiled at me happily; she, too, had noticed just how stunning Mary was.

I felt some relief when I realized Charles wasn't with them. With him out of the picture, things would be far less complicated and risky, and I would have a better chance at getting some alone time with Mary without him sniffing around like the dog he was.

Everybody enjoyed their time, talking about their businesses and lives while sipping on drinks and nibbling on food brought by the waiters. As the host, I made sure to mingle with all my guests. I wasn't arrogant about it, but deep down, I couldn't believe that in a matter of just a few years, a farm kid was to the point of hosting an elaborate party for the elite of Baghdad.

I planned to speak with Mary after lunch, and everything was moving along accordingly. I often stole looks at her while I mingled, and I noticed that she was looking right back at me.

I was standing next to General Thompson, talking with him about his garden, when I was joined by Mr. Radhi, Mr. Philipe, my French guest, and Dr. Kamal.

74

Dr. Kamal had come from a wealthy family, a long line of doctors. They had no interest in politics, it seemed, but Dr. Kamal's trip to Russia had intrigued him. He was impressed by the Russian ideologies and theories, so he enjoyed talking about politics in that regard. He was very straightforward and did not mince words, even though his views differed from those of most of the people who were present. He spoke a lot about socialism and the importance of community; it became very clear very quickly that the good doctor was a communist at heart. At that time, Iraq was a very unstable nation, swarming with various movements and beliefs and mindsets, all battling against one another. Some Iraqis were content and happy with Prime Minister Nuri Al Said or Nuri Pasha as he was called and the royal family, while others were nationalists, communists, or Baathists who weren't. Everyone had different visions for Iraq, and the ongoing situation with Egypt, Israel, France, and Britain only fueled that sometimes hostile division in the country.

During our conversation, Dr. Kamal was very open about many issues. He acknowledged the vast differences among the Iraqi population, but he also mentioned that a very small percentage of the public was enjoying life to its fullest potential. He said that too many of the elite cared only about themselves while the majority of the society was suffering from lack of employment, food, and education. The doctor ranted on about the need for unions in the various workforces and industries so that workers would be better represented and their requirements and needs better met. Mainly, Dr. Kamal talked about Iraq's reaction to Egypt's nationalization of the Suez Canal Company, specifically to Egyptian President Gamel Abdul Nasser.

Dr. Kamal spoke of a story about British Prime Minister Eden having dinner with King Feisal II and Nuri Pasha of Iraq when he received news of Egypt's decision to nationalize the Suez Canal Company. Apparently, Nuri Pasha himself advised Eden to hit Gamel right away and "show him the iron fist." Incensed about the matter, Dr. Kamal emphasized, "It is an absolute shame that an Iraqi prime minister would advise that his Arabic brother should be killed, and this proves that the current government's loyalty is far from what the people in the streets desire." He went on and on about this topic to anyone who would listen and spoke very loudly about the matter, not caring who overheard him.

Of course none of this sat well with General Thompson, as he had a different take on the matter. He adamantly defended the Iraqi government and attempted to explain why all their actions were in the best interest of Iraq and its people. He also requested patience. "The government is well aware, as am I, of the social and economic division of the people here, but it does take time to mend these things. The wheels are already turning to create a more closely knit society. In a matter of years, equality will exist for all Iraqis in regard to social standing and access to work and education."

Views continued to be exchanged, and the more the talk droned on, the more guests gathered. Dr. Kamal

76

seemed to be getting the upper hand in the argument, as his points and questions were echoed among the people present, and the general had little to say in response to many of the points the doctor wisely brought up.

Then, from out of nowhere, Charles suddenly appeared. He rudely pushed his way into the conversation, but he had little to offer other than curses and foul words against anyone who opposed the current Iraqi regime. Clearly, he'd been listening in, because he insisted on arguing and being rude. Not only did Charles interrupt Dr. Kamal with his nonsensical remarks about the problems in Iraq, but he went completely out of line when he began to personally insult the doctor. He began by scolding him for preaching communism, then immaturely began to insult the doctor's taste in clothes. In a matter of minutes, his uneducated, rude, and stupid verbal attack on the doctor turned the entire conversation into a tense battle, to the point where the two men had to be physically restrained and separated.

I managed to pull Charles aside and said, "Please calm down, Charles. This is a party, and I ask that you respect all of my guests. The general and the doctor were simply having a discussion, and both are entitled to their opinions, even if they disagree."

Charles was out of control and drunk; I could smell the alcohol on his breath every time he spoke. To make matters worse, he was an angry drunk who was in a very bitter mood, likely suffering from a hangover from the night before. When I couldn't calm him down, the general tried to escort him out. Charles cursed loudly and yelled at Dr. Kamal in drunken slurs, "Maybe you need a lesson like the one Fahd had to learn in 1949!"

Fahd, whose real name was Yusuf Salman Yusuf, was one of the early founders of the communist party in Iraq, a very outspoken activist. He was arrested for inciting riots and publicly speaking out in favor of communism, only to be executed on February 14, 1949 by the orders of Nuri Pasha.

When Charles made that threat on one of my esteemed guests, I had no option but to act quickly to force him to leave the grounds. Mustafa and I pulled him away and demanded that he leave immediately, before we had to throw him out and humiliate him.

To avoid further embarrassment, Charles left of his own free will, but before his departure, he whispered several threats to me. "I won't forget this, Ali, and I will get my revenge on you for humiliating me like this in front of the general and Mary," he wailed.

I'd had an uncomfortable feeling about him from the first moment I'd seen him, and I knew he was going to cause trouble. The way he behaved at my party proved that I'd been right about him all along.

After Charles left, everything returned normal, and no one dared discuss politics any further. I had never cared anything about politics. Even if Iraqi society was divided, all I wanted to do was live a happy, normal life, surrounded by family and friends that I could trust, enjoying my work and getting by day by day.

An hour later, the general took me aside. He was very apologetic about the whole fiasco Charles had created and assured me that it would not happen again.

"Do not mention it," I assured him. "It was not your fault, General, and I just want you to enjoy the party."

The lunch menu had been very carefully selected by Madam Laila. I stood up on the roof for a bit, overlooking my guests down below as they dined. Everyone seemed to delight in the food and looked satisfied.

I quickly noticed that Mary was alone, eating by herself, so I went down to talk to her. I had so much to say, and I hoped I would remember it all. "Mary, after the second song, can you excuse yourself to use the washroom and head to the other side of the house, in the direction of the nursery? I've left the gate open, and I will be waiting. Don't worry about Naseema, I have everything under control," I said quietly to her.

Without a word, she smiled and nodded her approval, then daintily dabbed at the corners of her mouth with a napkin.

I took Mustafa aside so we could go over my plans one more time. I would take Mary to the corner of my nursery so I could talk with her. Mustafa was more than willing to serve as a lookout, in case anyone walked from the back garden to the front, where my nursery was. Although I doubted that anyone would leave their places, extra care was needed to ensure that I'd have my privacy with Mary.

Mustafa had suggested we bring an Iraqi Maqam band, a band consisting of a Quanun player strumming an old, Arabic harp, a drummer, and an oud player with someone singing Iraqi poems in beautiful harmony. I agreed with him that the live band could play after lunch and for the remainder of the party, as it would keep all of the guests distracted and engaged and give me the time I needed with Mary.

Madam Laila was part of the plan as well; she was asked to occupy Miss Naseema in one way or another so she wouldn't feel compelled to tag along when Mary came to speak with me. Although Naseema seemed to have a nice heart and I thought she could eventually be convinced that my love for Mary was pure, I felt it was too soon to tell her. I was sure it would only take fifteen minutes for me to tell Mary what I had to say, so it would be easy enough for Laila to entertain Naseema for that short amount of time.

The Maqam band began playing as planned, and most of the Iraqi guests sang along. The foreigners enjoyed that little taste of Iraqi culture as much as the Iraqis did, and they shared in the action by clapping and dancing. Everyone seemed happy and distracted, so as soon as the first song finished, I left and gave Madam Laila a look.

A few minutes later, my Mary joined me. I was about to say the words I had carefully selected, but out of nowhere, she spoke first. "Ali, if you promise me that you'll never hurt me, shout at me, or leave me alone—if you'll promise that you'll always love me—I-I will be yours." A tear rolled down her left cheek as the last words left her mouth.

I was speechless, left in complete shock. Not one of the scenarios that had been playing through my mind had involved Mary giving herself to me so freely. I had no idea that Mary would take the initiative and start the conversation. I quickly took out a handkerchief, moved closer to that sweet, delicate, lovely flower of a woman, and wiped away her tears. When I could finally speak again, I said, "Not only do I promise that, but I also promise that I will dedicate my life to your happiness. You are my life, Mary, and I would never hurt you." After she smiled and looked up at me with tear-filled green eyes, I realized I still had some things to tell her. I was sure Mary wasn't naïve, but I wanted to be sure she saw the full picture, that she realized from the outset that things would be very complicated for us. "Mary, are you sure?" I asked her several times. "It will be very difficult for us to be together, and most of the world and the people we know will be against us. I'm willing to fight the world for you, Mary, but you have to know it is not going to be easy. The rosebush of our relationship will be very, very beautiful, but it will also come with thorns."

"I know," she said quietly.

"I love you, Mary, but are you really, really sure you're ready to—"

She stopped me from continuing and put her left hand on my chest, hovering just over my heart. "Ali, my love, as long as we are together, no one can stop us. Meet me tomorrow at the cloth market at four p.m., near a shop called Abu Abbas, and we will spend some time together." She then excused herself, for fear that everyone might begin to wonder where she was. Before she went, she thanked me for the way I had handled Charles. "He can be quite a monster sometimes. I am glad you asked him to leave." Then, just like that, my beautiful little bird fluttered away.

I didn't go back to the party right away because I wanted to savor the moment.

A few minutes later, I was joined by Mustafa, who gave me the most curious look. "Well? How did it go, cousin?" he asked when I said nothing.

I looked at him with a dreamy expression on my face and said, "I-I feel alive, Mustafa. I don't think I've ever felt so happy, and I was right about her. She wants me as well, and I cannot tell you how much it means to me to know that."

We then sat silently for a few minutes, just basking in the moment and listening to the guests as they sang along with the Maqam band, and finally made our way back to the party after a while.

All the guests left around six p.m. With the exception of Dr. Kamal's and Charles's argument, everything had gone smoothly, and everyone had had an unforgettable good time. I thanked Mr. Radhi and Madam Laila for all their hard work that had made the party a success.

On his way out, my uncle hugged me tightly. "I'm so proud of you, Ali. If your father was still alive, he'd be the happiest, proudest father in all of Baghdad."

Those words meant a lot to me as I looked up to the skies…

✻ ✻ ✻

At that point, Adnan stopped reading. He put the book and his notebook aside and just stared out the window for a few minutes before he broke into a small fit of laughter—not a joyous laugh but a sarcastic one, a chuckle of sadness as he stared at the dark streets of Baghdad. "Ah, my fair city, it has always been the same for you, hasn't it? Even in that era, when Ali was making your gardens beautiful, you could not find peace. Even then, you were divided. Will this ever end? Will the people of Iraq ever be united so there can be real beauty in our world?"

He then took a deep breath and decided to go out for a little walk. He picked a kebab sandwich for dinner and warmed a glass of tea, then settled in for a long night of reading.

# Chapter 4

Adnan missed his wife and her cooking, but the kebab wasn't bad. Besides that, it was the last night he would spend in his shop before everything went back to normal. After finishing his quick dinner and his tea and wiping his mouth and hands so as not to smudge the precious pages, he opened the book and continued reading...

⁎⁎⁎

I wore a nice gray suit decorated with a small white rose when I went to the market to meet Mary, and I arrived there at a quarter till four. I only had to inquire with one person about the location of the Abu Abbas shop, as everyone knew the biggest, oldest clothing shop in the area. Abu Abbas was around seventy years of age, and he had taken over the store after his father passed away. It had been passed down to his father from his grandfather and so on. The store was over 100 years old, and it had an outstanding reputation due to its history and because they sold all types of cloth and garments from all over the world, including Persia, Turkey, Japan, China, Kashmir, and even Europe.

I was standing inside the place when Mary sneaked up on me from behind, a welcome surprise. "Don't worry," she said. "Miss Naseema is far away, busy bargaining with another shopkeeper as she always does." She smiled as if she was very glad to see me and asked, "How are you, Ali?"

"Well, I haven't been able to sleep because I keep thinking of you."

"Really? I've never slept better. Maybe it's because I've been so happy and so excited about seeing you today."

After that, we remained silent for a few moments and let our eyes do all the talking. Her expression was so sincere and shy; she only gazed into my eyes for a few seconds before smiling and turning away or batting her eyes at the ground, then looked back up at me again. I, on the other hand, never took my eyes off of her. In my eyes, I hoped she could see that I was a man deeply in love, a man who couldn't believe I was fortunate enough to be there with a woman like her. I still couldn't believe that the most beautiful lady in Baghdad was there with me, Ali, a simple gardener. The more I thought about it, the harder it was to believe: Of all the men in the world, she had chosen me.

Even though the market was teeming with people bustling about everywhere, I couldn't hear a sound. Everything around me seemed to melt into silence as I stood there admiring Mary's unique beauty, only enhanced by all of the lush, colorful fabrics that surrounded her. It was as if I was standing in another galaxy, a place where multicolored lights illuminated everything and warmed me to my core. We both simply looked at each other, standing there in silence, for what seemed like the longest time.

After a few minutes, I broke the quietness and admitted, "Mary, not only am I the happiest man in the world, but I'm also the luckiest. I am surrounded by gorgeous blossoms and lovely, soft petals every day, yet I've never seen anything as beautiful and delicate as you, and I know I will never see anything so beautiful in my whole life that even comes close." I went on to tell her that I'd been dreaming for months about her, fantasizing about us being together, and wondering what I would say if given the chance. "These little clandestine rendezvous are nice, Mary, but I have to see you more often. It is so hard to spend my days apart from you. We need to arrange to meet as often as we can."

"I can see you again in just six days. On Tuesday, Miss Naseema and Mr. Dalton always go to the butcher to buy meat for the house, and they also run other errands. They should be gone by ten a.m., and they'll be away from the house for at least two hours. My father isn't in Baghdad right now, so that means I'll be alone with the maids. I'll leave your name with the gatekeepers so you can drop by. If anyone asks, you can simply say you're checking on the garden."

"Don't worry about anyone being suspicious," I assured her with a gentle pat on the hand. "I have another client in the compound, and I'll arrange to visit him on Tuesday afternoon. That way, our story will be covered from every angle."

We exchanged deep looks before she told me she had to leave. Just as she was about to walk away, I grabbed a piece of purple satin from behind her and asked the shopkeeper how much it was. I gave the man the money he requested, then placed the satin over her hair. Purple was definitely her color and looked amazing on her. Mary was a shy woman and blushed. She smiled but couldn't bear to look me in the eyes as she thanked me and went on her way, caressing the satin scarf I'd given her.

Mary had made a wise decision to meet at Abu Abbas because it was always crowded, everybody was busy bargaining, and no one even noticed the other customers. After she left, I remained there for ten minutes, watching Mr. Abbas as he bargained and joked with his customers. He was full of life and clearly loved working in the store, his family's heritage, and the sight and sound of his boisterous laughter gave me hope that life could be happy and good. After I left the shop, I bought a cup of tea at the market and made my way back home.

⁝⸲⸲

Ever since I'd hosted the party at my home, it had become a custom for several of my party guests to stop by in the evenings for tea and talks. The regulars included men from all walks of life: Mr. Radhi; Mr. Adeeb, a journalist; Mr. Akram, a well-known painter; and Mr. Danial, a math teacher. We usually sat by the river and played dominoes while we talked. I wasn't that interested in politics, but it was the common topic of conversation in those days, as a great majority of people were quite fed up with the British influence in Iraq, fearing that our country might lose its Arabic identity. The complaints about this matter were becoming more and more prevalent in the streets.

During one of those talks, Mr. Adeeb mentioned that many people in southern Iraq weren't that keen on the prime minister and the British anymore. Every day, he received reports from his colleagues about demonstrations held to protest the poor living conditions.

I tried to focus on their words, but I couldn't stop thinking about Mary. I worried that if the bitterness against the British escalated, she and her father and their companions would be forced to leave Iraq to go back to the UK. *Where would that lead us?* I thought. I was glad we were set to meet in just two days, as we had much to talk about, particularly considering everything I'd heard from my visitors.

⁂

Everything went smoothly when I went to meet Mary on Tuesday. I had no problems passing through the main gate of the compound, and I reached the Thompson residence around ten after ten. I found Mary in the garden, dressed in white pants and a long-sleeved green shirt; it was the first time I'd seen her in trousers, and the well-fitting garments only confirmed that she was a carefully sculptured angel. She greeted me in a normal

88

way, as if I was merely her gardener, so as not to arouse the suspicions of any nosy people in her household. We acted very natural, as if I was just there to do my job and check the gardens.

When we finally sat down at the end of the back garden, near the strawberries, she told me she was very pleased with them. She also mentioned that she enjoyed picking the tiny red fruits. "I love them!" she said. "They're so good and sweet, just like you, Ali."

Mary was much more open this time. We talked mainly about her and how she coped with being a daughter of a military man. She said she never really felt at home anywhere. She also told me about her time in England, where she studied literature, and she said she had a strong desire to study more in that field. It was fascinating to hear her talk about her life, and whenever she told me about her experiences, I closed my eyes for a second and tried to imagine her in those moments of her life.

It was obvious that she cared greatly for Naseema and Mr. Dalton, and she praised them for always being there for her. Much like me, Mary was a broken soul, a person who longed for the care she'd missed out on when she'd lost her mother at an early age to death and had lost her father to his military commitments. It was somewhat similar to my story, so we were connected in that way, and I understood how she felt. In fact, I could almost feel every word she said rather than just hearing them.

During our talks, I often referred to "Inshallah." Because Mary had spent years in Egypt and in Baghdad, she had heard it a lot and understood its meaning: "If God desires." She enjoyed learning Arabic words and asked me to speak in my native language, and I was happy to comply.

Our time went by far too fast, but she promised that she would stop by the nursery soon, as she needed some things for her garden.

"I can't wait to see you again, Mary," I said. "I miss you already." I also warned her to be very careful when going out, as things weren't very stable in Baghdad. I didn't want to worry her, but I wanted her to be cautious.

⁛⁛⁛

I wouldn't see Mary for another week, so I occupied myself with my work on the many projects I had. At that time, several gardens needed to be redesigned, two of them in the compound where Mary lived. I was also bombarded with other work orders on a daily basis. My business was booming, expanding so fast that I had to bring in four more people to help. I was ordering more seeds and was working more hours than ever before, but I was thankful for it. It was my only distraction, something to take my mind off of Mary, because the time apart from her was torture.

I remember Mary arrived around six p.m. one day with Mr. Dalton. She told him it was okay for him to do as he pleased, because she'd need at least an hour and a half to look through the garden for some flowers, and she wanted to have some tea at the fountain and enjoy the place for a while. Mr. Dalton thought it was an excellent idea, since he preferred to run his errands alone, so he left Mary at my nursery and assured her he'd be back before dark.

As soon as he left, Mary and I took a walk toward my back garden that overlooked the river. I asked her if she'd ever taken a boat ride along the Tigris, or any other river.

"No, not in Baghdad," she said. "I took a boat ride in Cairo with my father, Mr. Dalton, and a bunch of Father's friends, but it wasn't enjoyable. All they did was talk about politics and war. After that, I'm not sure I'm too keen on boat rides."

"I'm sure I can change your mind," I said. "Can I take you for a short ride?"

She was reluctant at first, but I assured her that it would take only a half-hour, and we had plenty of time before Mr. Dalton returned. When I asked her to trust me, any doubts she had evaporated right away. "Uh, sure," she said. "I'll take a boat ride with you, Ali."

I quickly went inside and ran to the bedroom, where I had a new abaya, still wrapped, stashed in one of the drawers. It was nice to see Mary in the abaya, a black cloth commonly worn by Iraqi women. I asked her to place it over her head and clothes and to head over to my boat. Meanwhile, I rushed back to the nursery and told my workers, "I have some things to tend to. If anyone comes looking for me, tell them I'll be back shortly."

I knew that those moments would never be erased from my mind, not till I took my last breath on Earth. Mary looked absolutely unforgettable in the abaya, with her golden hair blowing in the cool breeze and an innocent smile that never seemed to leave her face. I knew I'd .never forget the sun setting in the background with Mary in the frame; it was the perfect scene, like one might imagine when reading a romance novel. She stood at the front of the boat, enjoying the natural beauty of the Tigris and the reflection of the sun on the water. For the entire twenty minutes, neither of us uttered a single word; again, our eyes spoke on our behalf. I couldn't help admiring her beauty while she was transfixed on some other world, a world that seemed peaceful and happy.

We got back in time for her to select a few flowers and have tea with me for thirty minutes before Mr. Dalton arrived to pick her up. Before she left, she turned to me and whispered, "*Shukran,*" thanking me in Arabic.

I grabbed her gently by the arm, played with her beautiful hair, and said, "Thank you, Mary. From now on, you will have a surprise every day on your balcony".

She walked behind Mr. Dalton and laughed loudly as they walked to the car.

Mary truly did love the surprises, a special rose placed every day on her balcony, sometimes a red one, sometimes pink, and sometimes another hue—and every one not nearly as spectacular as the young woman I gave them to.

As my work in the compound flourished, the security guards grew to know me well. I was given a monthly pass, as it became tiring for them to go through the same security routine when I visited several times a week. Once I had the monthly pass, whether I had business there or not, I walked to the back of Mary's house and threw a rose, tied to a small rock to give it some weight, onto her balcony. My childhood games with Mustafa, throwing stones into glass bottles for hours, helped ensure that I'd never miss my target.

For the next five weeks, things remained the same. Mary and I met in the market sometimes, or I visited her home when Mr. Dalton and Miss Naseema were away. Sometimes, she dropped by the nursery. We never spent more than an hour or two together, and the time flew by too quickly. We both felt a need to see each other more and more, and every one of our encounters felt painfully shorter than the last. It was as if we were watching an hourglass, the sands of time moving far too quickly as each of our precious together moments slipped by.

We never felt comfortable and safe sitting together, and we were always on the lookout for onlookers, checking here and there and constantly on alert. We were careful not to be seen too close to one another, and we didn't take any risks. We were both aware of the devastating consequences of being caught, so we were very careful not to let that happen to us.

Still, as cautious as we had to be, we cherished every minute we spent with each other, and we lived each day in the hopes of seeing one another again. Every time we met was like the first time, and our shared happiness and passion were never fading. We talked about everything, including our pasts and our wishes for the future, and in only a few short weeks, we knew every little detail about one another.

For weeks, Mary had been promising to give me a surprise, something pleasant that she would only reveal to me at the right time. When that time came, I realized the surprise was well worth waiting for. We were at Abu Abbas's shop, a place where we'd met many times before, and Mary was looking at something she really liked. She told me she would love to buy it, but just as I was about to ask one of the sellers about the price, Mary began talking instead—in perfect Arabic! I couldn't believe my ears. Her voice carried a slight accent, but she spoke the words well and with much confidence. I listened as she bargained with the shopkeeper, and after she'd purchased her cloth and we left the shop, I gave her a confused, shocked look.

She said in Arabic, "Eight weeks, Ali. I've been studying for eight weeks, four hours a day. It isn't fair that we always have to communicate in my language and not yours. The next time we meet, we will talk only in Arabic. Wait for me at the nursery on Wednesday, in about four days. I'll drop by around ten in the morning."

After she left, I was still in complete disbelief but happy as could be. Shaking my head and smiling, I walked

94

slowly past a carpet shop and ran into Dr. Kamal there. I had seen him only once since my party, when he'd collided with Charles, and it had been two months since we'd sat at the same café together with some of our friends.

"Why, hello, Ali," he greeted. He then proceeded to tell me he'd been very busy, but he wanted to talk to me and asked if we could find a quiet place to sit.

We walked a few streets to a café near the post office, one I'd visited several times before. It was a nice, quiet place, and most of the patrons were writers or poets.

Dr. Kamal soon began talking of his favorite topic: how the impoverished Iraqis in the general population were struggling and starving while the royal family and the Iraqi parliament did nothing about it. Not wanting to discuss something so grim and dull, I tried to change the subject, but he finally began asking me more personal questions. Knowing I wasn't originally from Baghdad, he asked about my family back in Diyala. "What education is available?" he asked. "Are there better services than in Baghdad?"

In an effort to be honest about what little I knew of such things, I replied, "They are certainly not on par with Baghdad, and improvement is needed there as well as everywhere else."

Dr. Kamal shook his head, and a sad look came over his face. "Ali, things are worse in other places, but I had to see it to believe it. It's time for a change in our country. Royalty is no longer a feasible option. The young

95

people in Iraq know that, and there are movements stirring up. Our country desperately needs to find its Arabic pride once again," he said. "We must rediscover what we've lost along the way, what made Baghdad and all of Iraq so great till now." He turned and looked at me with a solemn expression on his face. "You, Ali, are still young, yet you have done very well for yourself and are quite an inspiration. You could have some influence on others, and I'd like you to be part of this important movement."

I wasn't sure what to say to him, but I became even more concerned and uneasy when he said he wanted to arrange a secret meeting with some people from communist party. As soon as I heard that, I thanked him for his time and excused myself, not wanting to discuss the matter further. I was a man of plants and trees and flowers, not of politics, and while I knew there was instability in the country, I didn't believe it was my role to do anything about it. I, like most Iraqis at the time, knew things had to change, and I believed they would in time, but I was certain those negotiations were better left in the hands of politicians and figureheads who knew far more about the political unrest than I did. I didn't believe Dr. Kamal or the communists would be willing to be patient, to give the much-needed time for changes to happen, and I didn't agree with his approach. I politely asked Dr. Kamal never to speak to me about it again, and after I paid for our tea, we walked away from the café.

After we'd taken only a few short steps, much to my misfortune, we passed General Thompson and

Charles, who seemed to be on their way to the post office. Everyone was civil and exchanged casual greetings, but even though it was a brief encounter that would have been quickly ended, Charles, the serpent that he was, insisted on leaving some of his poison everywhere.

"Dr. Kamal and Ali! Are you out here trying to change the future?" he boomed in a mocking, loud voice intended to humiliate us. "It will not happen in your lifetimes, gentlemen...and if I were you, I'd be careful what you say and to whom you say it."

Dr. Kamal replied back sarcastically, "Changes may happen sooner than you might imagine, Charles"

As soon as the two exchanged their hostile words and threats, we all went our own way. It was a very disturbing encounter that continuously ran through my head, and if I could have changed one day in the history of my life, that would have been the day. Had I known what I was going to run into that day, I would have gone another way when I'd left Mary at the clothing store. I wished I hadn't bumped into Dr. Kamal, and I certainly did not want to see Charles and the General. In hindsight, I suppose it was my destiny; the awkward meeting simply had to happen.

I went to visit Mr. Radhi that same day. I told him what had happened and reiterated what Dr. Kamal had said about the feelings of the general population in Iraq.

Mr. Radhi anticipated that it would be only a matter of time before the Iraqi situation escalated. He had heard from several close friends that many agreed there was a need for change, and several thought Iraq should side with Egypt. He advised me to avoid such confrontations with Dr. Kamal and anyone who had such ideas. "This is not the time for them," he said. "Yes, changes need to be made, but not through those methods. Also, you must be careful of that conniving, meddling, hotheaded Charles. He seems to be quite a snake in the grass."

As he'd promised, Mr. Radhi did not say anything negative about my relationship with Mary, but I could see in his eyes that he was still concerned, primarily for my safety and wellbeing. Still, he was an honorable man, true to his word, and even though he knew I was heading for trouble by secretly meeting up with Mary, he kept those discouraging thoughts to himself.

When Wednesday came, I told Mary about what had happened. She already knew I'd seen Charles, because the day before, he'd had dinner at their house, and they had talked about communism. Charles had made sure to mention that he'd seen me and "the communist doctor." She was bothered by the fact that Charles had mentioned more than once that Mary and those in her household should move out of Iraq, as things seemed to be heading in a wrong direction. In fact, several times during that meal, he'd mentioned to the general that he was ready to marry her. "Finally, when I grew tired of his nonsense," she said, "I shouted, 'Never!' and excused myself from the table." There was something different about that meeting with her that had me unsettled. A sadness had seeped into her amazing green eyes, and it was obvious that she was being put under a lot of pressure from her father to wed Charles.

"Don't worry," I assured her. "I'll never let that happen, not while I'm alive."

The only upside of the meeting, other than the fact that I was able to look at the love of my life, was that I loved every Arabic word Mary was speaking, and she spoke Arabic nearly all the time.

⁘⁘⁘

Some events in life are so monumental that we remember the exact time and place where we were when they happened. October 29, 1956 is an example of that for me. I had just walked out of my home, and I was dressed very dapperly in my new black, pinstriped suit, off-white shirt, and a white rose in my jacket pocket. I was humming *"Salou Qalbi"* ("Ask My Heart") by Um Kalthoum, one of the greatest Arab singers. I noticed that many people were gathering around a radio outside of Abu Khalid's café, which was only a short walk from my home. As I drew nearer to the crowd, I overheard the people arguing. I listened closely to the reports on the radio and quickly realized what all the fuss was about: Egypt was under attack by Israel mainly in response to the nationalization of the Suez Canal Company and other reasons, and France and Britain had given Abdul Nasser an ultimatum.

My first thoughts were on Nuri Pasha, our prime minister, and I wondered what his response would be to the Suez Canal crisis. I wondered what the impact of his decision would be on the Iraqi people, many of whom were already bitterly angry with the Iraqi government and its lack of Arabic nationalism. I also wondered how all of it would impact the safety of foreigners in Iraq, particularly Mary and her family and friends, who would likely be considered enemies to the Arab world.

I skipped work that day and headed straight over to see Mr. Radhi, my wise mentor. He was absolutely furious about the news and was worried about the consequences. Mr. Radhi was certain that Egyptian President Abdul Nasser would refuse to accept the British and French terms; it only made common sense that no president would, as it would simply be all the excuse the French and British would need to attack Egypt. Mr. Radhi could tell that I was worried about Mary. "Ali, if you truly love her, you must convince her to leave as soon as possible. It is not safe for her and her loved ones here. Nuri Pasha, will publicly announce that he sides with the British, and that will make the Iraqi people very upset with all Brits, Mary and her father and friends included."

I left his place feeling more worried than I'd ever been. I needed some inside news, as the radio reports were very vague and general. I knew where to go for the details and the real facts: none other than Duraid, the local barber. Duraid was a short, chubby man in his late fifties; since he'd already lost most of his own hair, he had no problem cutting the hair of others. Prior to that, he'd worked as a neighborhood dentist as well, and many trusting parents brought their little ones to Duraid. At that time, it was customary for barbers to do some dental work, but once the regulations changed, Duraid could only work as a barber full time.

The barber loved to talk, and from the moment someone entered his shop till the moment they left, he would talk their ear off. He knew everyone in the local area; his clientele included officers, journalists, teachers, and common folk from all parties, be they communists, nationalists, Baathists, or socialists. If there was any news to tell or any rumors to be heard, Duraid's barbershop was the place to hear it.

I timed my visit carefully and made sure to arrive just as his shop was getting to close for his afternoon break and all customers had left the shop. I explained that I was in a hurry to get to an important meeting and that I needed a nice shave.

The barber was a bit reluctant, but then he cleaned the chair and said, "Hop on up here, and I will see what I can do." Within a minute, the talkative clipper started talking about the morning news, telling me everything he knew about the war and the impact it was already having on the people.

According to Duraid, things were even worse in Iraq than we had imagined. An Iraqi officer who had visited him earlier in the morning had told him that three British soldiers had been killed several days prior, while on their way back to Al Habbaniya Air Base, just west of Baghdad. The British claimed it was a misfortunate road accident, but the Iraqi officer adamantly accused them of lying. "It was no accident," he'd told Duraid. "Their car was full of bullets holes. They were attacked and shot to death." Duraid said that when he asked the Iraqi officer how he knew that, the officer claimed that his source was a British major he often had tea with.

"And that's not the first incident or the last," Duraid said as he continued to shave my chin. "With this war afoot, I reckon the attacks will surely increase. The streets are on fire, my young friend, and the people have had enough."

Once he was finished with my shave, I thanked him, paid him, and left. I knew Mr. Radhi and Duraid were right: It wasn't safe any longer, and the problems would only escalate. As much as I hated the idea, my Mary would have to leave—at least for a while. I could hardly bear to be apart from her, but I certainly didn't want any harm to come to her.

The security around the foreigners' compound that day was tighter, and the number of soldiers on guard had tripled. Nevertheless, I had no trouble getting inside, since they all knew me as a common face who'd visited often. I just had to see Mary and warn her, and I didn't even bother making an excuse as to why I was there.

I stood outside and knocked on the door, and a second later, Mr. Dalton welcomed me in. I told him I had some work to do within the compound but wanted to check on the Thompsons to make sure they were all right.

Mr. Dalton asked me if I'd heard the news, and I told him what I knew and mentioned that I was concerned for their safety. "Yes, I know, Ali," he said.

"The general is even very tense, and I have never seen him like that before. He has instructed us to pack quickly for an emergency leave. Of course, Mary doesn't want to go and has been arguing with him about it for hours."

The news from Mr. Dalton was bittersweet. On one hand, I was sad to see Mary go, and my heart ached at the thought. At the same time, I took some relief in knowing she would be safe. Regardless of my feelings for her, she had to leave. She had to be safe, and those were hard times in Baghdad for foreigners.

A few minutes later, Mary came to see me, and Mr. Dalton excused himself. Her eyes were bloodshot from crying so much, and she immediately burst into tears again and began bellowing, stating that she didn't want to leave Iraq. "I don't want to leave you, Ali! I just found you, and I'm not ready to lose you now."

Every word she said tore at my heart, and I had to really struggle to fight back my emotions. "Sit down, Mary," I said gently, "and let me talk this through with you." Once she'd calmed down a little, I got straight to the point. "Mary, no matter where we are in the world, no matter how far apart, we will always be together. Our souls are one, and not even life and death can separate us. You must be wise, my darling. It is not safe to stay here, and your father is right in saying you should take your leave while you still can. The Iraqi people are angry, and they will release that fiery anger on anyone whom they feel represents the war on Egypt. I know you have nothing to do with all of this, but because you are British, you will be in danger if you stay."

She burst into tears again, and I couldn't bear to see her that way. I quickly ushered her to the back of their house, next to the strawberry bed, and wiped her soft tears away. Looking into her eyes, I moved closer, and we shared our first kiss. It only lasted for seconds, but even two years later, I can still feel that kiss whenever I close my eyes and remember that moment. I felt my body flying with her, away from everything. It was as if we were floating in the clouds, enjoying our own world, our own place, something we never had on Earth. That kiss alone would have sustained me for a lifetime, and I would forever cherish the feel of her soft lips against mine.

The next day, as expected the British and French joined in the aggression, and Nuri Pasha, our prime minister, ignored the people's desire. He was clearly on the side of the British, turning his back on Egypt and the entire Arab world. Personally, I thought that while Nuri exercised bad judgment at the time, he truly believed that was in the best interest of Iraq. Only time would tell if he'd done right by his country or not, but no matter what decision he'd made, it would have negatively impacted my situation with Mary. If he had sided with the Arabs, the foreigners would have been forced to leave; if he sided with the British, which it appeared he had, it would be directly against the majority of the people's wishes including mine, and any British person in Iraq would be in danger of retribution.

Seemingly in an instant, turmoil and chaos boiled up in our beautiful country. The people were furious, and demonstrations broke out everywhere. Protests and strikes at schools and universities and in the streets made for a very hostile environment. Those who were not in the streets were glued to the radio, hoping to hear the latest news and cheering for every Egyptian victory, mourning every Egyptian loss.

Mary and Miss Naseema took their leave three days later. Saying goodbye so suddenly was painful, and even now, while writing about it, it stings. I do not like to recall that heartbreaking farewell, to relive that moment again. It was very hard on both of us. We embraced one another as tightly and for as long as we could, and when I finally let go of Mary, my jacket was soaked with her tears. They left Baghdad to Al Habbaniya Air base and left to London from there.

After ten days of fierce battles, the war was over. As is sometimes the case in wars, both sides claimed victory, though there were thousands of casualties all around. Egyptian radio stations played Arabic victory songs, while Israeli ones continued to blare out "*Hava Nagila.*" Meaning "Let us Rejoice." As a result of the war, British Prime Minister Eden resigned, and Russian influence in Egypt increased. As for Iraq, the strikes decreased, and things gradually began to calm down, but the divisions between the people and the government had only grown, and there was still a very thick tension in the air.

⁂

After three weeks, I received Mary's first letter, which she'd written just eight days after she'd left. With every word she'd poured out on the page, I felt her pain. She said she couldn't wait to see me and that the first week away had felt like the longest, most dreadful of her life. "The passing hours felt like years," she wrote, "and it was…unbearable." She also told me that Miss Naseema had encouraged her to take some poetry classes three times a week at a London university, hoping it would enable to take her mind off of her deep sadness. "It isn't helping, Ali, because even though I love poetry and love to learn, the last thing I remember before going to sleep every night is that I'm too far away from my real source of happiness. All I can do without you is cry."

I felt terrible reading that, and when I got the second letter nearly sixteen days later and read that she was still in misery and lonely, I knew I had to do something; I couldn't leave my darling Mary, the love of my life, languishing in pain while I just sat around, waiting and hoping for things to get better.

I went to Mr. Radhi and Madam Laila and told them I urgently needed to visit England. I was very honest with them and told them that I simply had to go to Mary, and I asked for their help to get me there. I knew Madam Laila, with her never-ending support of love and romance, would not allow Mr. Radhi to resist my pleas.

Thus, exactly eight days later, I found myself on a plane from Beirut to London. My only luggage was a small suitcase containing some clothes and a pair of shoes, and in my hand was a pendant, a gift for Mary. I had drawn the design myself, and one of Mustafa's gold crafters from abroad had helped to create the unique piece of jewelry, with two emerald stones that resembled Mary's magical eyes. There was even a place for a photograph to be inserted, and I could not wait to give it to Mary. There was only a week until Christmas, and I could not wait to give her the biggest holiday surprise of her life.

# Chapter 5

Adnan put the memoir down for a few minutes and looked at all the notes he'd scribbled so far in his black notebook. He'd made note of several events and the names he'd read. In red ink, he'd scrawled, "Ali, Radhi, Laila, Mustafa, and General Thompson." In blue ink, he'd written, "Naseema, Dr. Kamal, Charles, and Mr. Dalton." Beside each name, he'd written several additional notes.

After looking over his notes, collecting his thoughts, drinking some water, and taking a deep breath, he picked up the book and continued reading...

I arrived in London at nine a.m. The journey had taken me nearly two days, forty-four hours, from the moment I took the bus from Baghdad to Beirut, with only a few hours' rest in Syria and six hours overnight in Beirut. It was a hectic trip overall, but I knew Mary was well worth it.

I was wearing dark blue trousers, a white shirt, and a lighter blue jacket with the pendant tucked snugly in the inner pocket. I carried my brown suitcase in my left hand and the umbrella that Mr. Radhi had insisted I take in my right; he'd been right about the umbrella, because it was raining when I stepped out of the taxi at the airport, and during the week I spent there, it rained for six entire days.

Mr. Radhi had also recommended a nice, cozy bed-and-breakfast in Lambeth. He said it was close to the Waterloo railway station where I'd have to board the train to get to Mary's residence in Surrey. As always, Mr. Radhi's advice proved to be invaluable.

As soon as I reached my destination and got settled in, there were two things I had to do right away. First, I needed a good, clean shave, because I looked horrible with stubble on my face. Second, I had to purchase a proper hat; I was fond of hats and had many of my own, but my favorite, my Faisaliya, would have been out of place in the UK and made me stand out in a weird way.

The hotel receptionist, an elderly woman, was kind enough to help me with both. She informed me that the barber was only two blocks away, a short few minutes' walk. Although the barber was an old man like our barber back home, but unlike Duraid, he didn't speak much at all. During the course of my haircut and shave, he only said seven or eight words, asking how I wanted my hair, telling me how much it would cost, and bidding me goodbye when I left. The cultural differences were immediately evident.

As soon as I left the barbershop, I followed the directions the receptionist had told me, and I found the perfect shop in which to buy a hat. They had a decent collection of hats and scarves, and I quickly picked out a nice hat and put it on my head.

Once I left the hat shop, I walked around the corner and sat at a café, where I had some tea and tried to collect my thoughts and recall my plan for the next day.

It was good that Mary would be at the university when I met her, because there were several reasons why I didn't want to surprise her at home. First, she wasn't alone there, and I didn't want a confrontation with Miss Naseema to spoil the happy surprise. I also recalled that Mary's aunt, her father's sister, lived on the premises, and Mary had referred to her aunt as an "angrier version" of her father; of course I wanted no part of that.

My plan was to wait till nine thirty a.m., which would give Mary enough time to leave for the university. I would then drop by and visit Miss Naseema to forewarn her that I was there to surprise Mary with a visit. After all, she was like a mother to my Mary, and I had to convince her how sincere my feelings were and to make sure she was on my side. I already knew what to say, as I'd repeated it a hundred times over the course of my two-day journey. I had to make sure I had Miss Naseema's blessing, and if all went well with her, I would kindly ask her where Mary's university was. I could have found out for myself, as it would have been easy enough for me to follow Mary there, but I wanted to show some courtesy to Miss Naseema and make her feel as if she was an important part of our relationship. I really needed her, and it would make all the difference in the world to me and to Mary if I had her approval.

I left the café after an hour and walked around for a while, seeing the sights. I couldn't believe I was in London, a city I'd only imagined through the words of Charles Dickens or Shakespeare. I saw places and landmarks that I'd only read about in novels and plays: the River Thames, London Tower, the Tower Bridge, the Palace of Westminster, and Big Ben. It was absolutely breathtaking, and I loved every bit of it, but there was another place I had yet to see—a place Mr. Radhi had insisted that I visit, no matter what. "Go to the British Museum," he said. "You will learn more about the history of Iraq there than you ever will in Iraq itself."

When I got to the museum, I was stunned to discover what a great civilization Mesopotamia was, what a fascinating place I'd grown up in. There were sculptures from the Sumerian, Babylonian, and the Assyrian era, and some were amazingly intact. They were beautiful and absolutely mesmerizing, and I carefully examined every one and read all of the information about them. An hour earlier, I'd been enjoying the beauty of iconic structures in London, but the sculptures in that museum were thousands of years older and told me so much about my heritage and culture. *The Lamassu*, a winged bull with a human head, especially filled me with pride. It was such a magnificent structure, so delicately carved with great imagination and knowledge beyond our understanding.

I walked from one corridor to another and was nearly overwhelmed with the vast library, a collection of

Assyrian tablets. It was so emotional for me to look upon those old relics that my tears actually began to flow. Not only were my senses flooded with so much beauty, but I also felt sad. Most of the people back home had forgotten our origins. They had forgotten the achievements we had made throughout history and how we'd suffered under different occupations for centuries. I was heartbroken that our people were plotting against one another, individuals and groups trying to gain power, fame, and fortune instead of uniting for one cause, to help our nation rise up again to its rightful place in the world.

I left the museum with mixed feelings. Part of me was angry that our ancient treasures were in England and not in Iraq, the nation where they'd been forged, carved, and engraved. Then again, in London, our treasures were carefully looked after and shared with the world, something that I doubted would be possible in Iraq. Mr. Radhi wanted me to open my eyes and learn about our foundations. He wanted the youth of Iraq to understand from whence we'd come and build on that. Mr. Radhi was a great man who loved his great nation, and I couldn't thank him enough for all he'd done for me, including sending me to that museum.

I reached the bed-and-breakfast around six p.m. I was dead tired, and my legs felt like rubber. I took a warm bath and enjoyed a tasty homemade carrot soup for supper, something I'd never eaten before, courtesy of my hostess. Knowing I had a long and exciting day ahead of me, I excused myself shortly after dinner and quickly went to my room, curled up in the comfortable bed beneath the soft, daisy-scented covers, and fell asleep to the lullaby of the drizzling rain pitter-pattering against the window.

I slept for almost twelve hours, because I didn't wake up until the homeowner knocked on my door at six a.m., as I'd ask her to. She handed my clothes to me, freshly laundered and ironed, and informed me that breakfast was ready.

I took another delightful, refreshing, warm bath and dressed in the same clothes I'd worn on the flight; they carried the fresh smell of daisies, just like the blankets that had warmed me through the night.

Downstairs in the dining room, I had a small glass of fresh orange and a toast with butter and apricot jam. It wasn't a typical Iraqi breakfast, but Madam Laila often served it, so the tastes were familiar. The light breakfast was just enough to wake me up and get me started for the day.

I hopped on the train at eight fifteen, and the forty-five minute ride was not a pleasant one. A group of teenagers several seats away harassed and insulted me, calling me rude, bigoted names like "camel jockey" and "dark face." Clearly, they didn't appreciate people of darker complexions, especially those from the Middle East. At first I was furious and wanted to stand up and beat the hell out of them, but they were not worth jeopardizing my freedom and my chance to see Mary, so I concentrated on her beautiful face, her soft lips, and paid no further attention to the rubbish they spat. I refused to let anyone ruin my happy day. I was on my way to see Miss Naseema and then Mary, and nothing was going to spoil my mood. I tried to be strong and ignore them, but little did I know that it was only the first of much harassment I would face during my visit.

The Thompson residence wasn't far from Heathrow Airport, and once I arrived at the nearby railway station, I asked for the best way to get to Runnymede.

Mr. Radhi had told me to ask about Wentworth, a well-known golf club in the region, because the Thompson house was about a ten-minute walk from there, house number B-43. There were so many beautiful homes and estates near the golf club, and I carefully glanced at the house numbers until I found Mary's, the seventh one from the east side.

Their property was huge, possibly an acre or more, with beautiful views of the golf course. The home must have cost the general a fortune. Then entryway was constructed of beautiful brick and stone walls, and the walkway leading up to it was covered with small white stones. The gate was about three meters high, wrought iron and steel with a leaf design across the middle.

*This is it,* I thought to myself, a bit nervous. I took a deep breath and pulled the bell.

A young man, presumably in his early twenties, came to the gate a few seconds later. "Hello," he greeted with a hospitable smile. "Can I ask who you are and the nature of your business with the Thompsons?"

"I am a close family friend, from Baghdad, and I am here to discuss urgent business with Miss Naseema." I didn't want to give him my name, because I also wanted to take her by surprise. I wanted to be in control right from the start; if I could do that, the rest would be easy.

I had my back turned to the house when Miss Naseema came outside. "I am Naseema," she said, clearly not recognizing me. "How can I help you?"

I turned around slowly, took off my hat, gave her a slight smile. From that moment on, I had her. She didn't know what to say for a minute and was stunned into silence.

"May I come in?" I asked, breaking the ice.

Still speechless, she just motioned me inside with a wave of her hand. She led me to their garden, bigger than any I'd ever seen in Iraq.

The lawn was brilliant green, like perpetual spring, speckled with flowers in every color of the rainbow. The leafless trees had shiny, wide trunks, and one of them was so wide that I assumed it had to be at least 150 years old; it had probably been there way before they'd first constructed the estate. In addition to the large trees, there were several statues and sculptures to look at, mostly of Roman origin and design. The place certainly had potential, but some of the décor was hideous and mismatched, and like their garden in Baghdad had been, it was unorganized and dull and lacked soul; in essence, it was nothing but some statues and flowers haphazardly placed in front of a grand, immaculate mansion that deserved to be surrounded by beauty.

The house was built with large, gray stone like the type used for castles. There were two strong, smooth, marble pillars, each around ten feet tall. The large windows were the type that could be opened from both sides, perfect for letting the fresh air circulate through the home. On the second floor, a long terrace stretched from one side of the house to the other, and it was furnished with several seats and a table. There were so many windows that I guessed the house had at least ten rooms. I could see the maroon curtains and even some fancy chandeliers through the open windows. My immediate impression was that the house was lovely, though not nearly as lovely as the girl who lived in it.

Miss Naseema led me to a table, where I sat down. She then hurried back inside without saying a word. A few minutes later, she returned, carrying a silver tray that held a dainty porcelain teapot and two china cups. She was still in shock and said nothing as she put the tray down, poured a cup for me and then for herself, and finally took a seat.

I took the first sip of tea and started talking. It seemed I spoke nonstop for a whole hour, without her ever saying a word. I went on and on about my childhood, my feelings, and how I knew Mary and I were meant for each other. "Every minute with her is precious," I said, "and I cannot breathe when she is gone."

Finally, Miss Naseema spoke up. "Ali, the moment you showed up here, I finally understood what she meant to you. You mustn't fear me or consider me an obstacle now, if you even did before. Your Aunt Naseema is on your side, and I want nothing but the best for Mary. You love her and would clearly be willing to do anything for her, and that is all I could ever ask for. I wasn't sure about you before, but now I am." She smiled and refilled her teacup. "Mary is at Whitelands College in Southfields. James, our driver, will be happy to take you, so please be on your way. Don't waste your time here while Mary is somewhere else. Go create another precious moment for yourselves, Ali...and with my blessing."

I thanked her and kissed her on the top of her forehead. From the very first moment I'd met Miss Naseema, I had known there was a soft heart beneath that hard, serious exterior that she used to so fiercely protect Mary. I asked her permission to select a rose from her garden.

She laughed. "You may take two if you wish," she said, "but only if you promise not to throw it on one of our balconies." She gave me a slight wink, and I realized she was always aware of my daily gifts to Mary back in Baghdad. "You are worlds away from home here, Ali," she warned before I left. "When you get to the college, ask for Pauline. She works in administration, and she will be very helpful," she said over her shoulder as she walked back inside to summon James.

I cut a beautiful red rose and carefully placed it in my right side pocket, and five minutes later, James and I were on our way to Southfields. I was so excited and happy as the car pulled out of the Thompson estate that I wanted to open the window and shout as loudly as I could, but I managed to refrain.

James was a tall, well-built black gentleman with wide eyes, a thick, well-trimmed mustache, and a very rounded chin. I was sure he'd have a thousand questions, but he didn't say a thing for the first fifteen minutes, other than to offer me a copy of the morning paper. I could read his eyes very well in the rearview mirror, and it was obvious that he wanted to know more about his passenger. He was a professional chauffeur, however, and he knew it wasn't appropriate to ask his guests personal questions, so he held his tongue.

Since James was reluctant to speak to me, I felt it was normal for travelers of any sort to talk to one another, so I opted to start the conversation by asking him about his service with the Thompsons. "How long have you been with the family?" I asked.

"About six years," he said quickly, as if he still wasn't sure it was appropriate to speak to me. When I smiled back at him encouragingly, he went on to tell me he only saw them once or twice a year.

I didn't go into my personal details, but I shared with him that I had met them in Baghdad and had known them for nearly two years. My excuse for being there was that I had some news from Baghdad, better delivered in person.

After he relaxed a bit, James wouldn't stop talking. He told me about Mary's college. "It was one of the first higher education institutes in the country. At first, only females were allowed, but Miss Mary told me that just last year, they started to offer admission to young men. The school took its name from its old location in Chelsea, from the Whitelands House." He went on to tell me about the newest building on the campus, and I found the ride with James to be very relaxing and very informative.

It was raining a bit when we finally reached the school, some thirty-five minutes from the Thompson estate. James asked if he should wait for me, but I told him not to bother. "Just come back at the normal time, when you're scheduled to pick Mary up," I said, knowing that would give me three hours. I thanked him for the ride and asked him if I could borrow the newspaper.

The campus was huge, and students in crisp, clean uniforms with nary-a-wrinkle were walking around here and there, some in groups, others as couples, and a few all by themselves. The women clearly outnumbered the men.

As I walked past the students, many of them looked at me strangely; they knew I was neither a student nor a native Brit. Nevertheless, I walked confidently to the administrative offices and asked the secretary if I could speak to Pauline. A few seconds later, she shuffled out to meet me. "Hello. I am Pauline," she said, offering her hand for a shake. "How can I help you today?"

"I am one of General Thompson's friends," I said, "and I have an urgent message for his daughter that must be given to her in person." When she looked at me skeptically, I elaborated, "Miss Naseema has many good things to say about you, ma'am, and she said you would help me find Mary, since I've never been to your fine campus before."

Pauline was only twenty-seven or twenty-eight, and she was very helpful. She glanced at a schedule and told me, "Mary is in a class now, but they will be dismissed in twenty-five minutes. I can show you around while you wait if you like."

"That would be wonderful," I said, always eager to see new things and hoping it would help the time pass quickly. I was so anxious and eager to see Mary that every minute crept by at a torturously slow pace.

Pauline was a proud alumnus of Whitelands. She'd graduated five years ago, and had only good things to say about the university. She showed me the classroom where Mary was, then led me to the lockers. "This one is hers," she said. "If you wait here, she should show up shortly. I'm sure she'll come here after class to put her books away."

She'd made things so much easier for me, so I thanked her and went outside for a few minutes, just to have a look at the place and make sure my plans were clear in my head. I waited a few minutes, until the hallway with the lockers was empty again, then went back inside. I wanted to do something special. The thin metal door of Mary's locker wouldn't have been hard to open, but I didn't want to risk making any noise or breaking it and getting Mary in trouble. All I needed to do was create a small gap, just big enough for me to throw the rose from Mary's garden inside. I pulled it gently, bit by bit, until there was a large enough opening to insert the rose. I could tell there were some books inside, so I just threw the rose on top of them. I then took the special, custom-made pendant out of my pocket and threw it inside as well, as close to the rose as I could so she couldn't possibly miss it. I carefully returned the locker door to its original state, and it looked exactly as it was before, as if no one had touched it.

I walked away from my locker and studied the path Mary would use to get from the classroom to her locker. I hid on the other side of the hall, where she wouldn't notice me. From that vantage point, I could watch her every move, and I couldn't wait to see the surprise on her face when she found the unexpected gifts in her locker.

The saying we had in Iraq about the English always being on time was true, because exactly twenty-five minutes after Pauline had told me Mary's class would finish, students started pouring out. I hid my face behind James's newspaper and waited for the only student I cared to see. Three minutes passed, then four, and most of the students had already dropped their belongings and textbooks off at their lockers and walked away. Finally, Mary approached her locker. The world seemed to freeze, and my heart began to jump in my chest. I could feel my shirt moving with every beat as I looked at her. *No wonder it rains all the time here,* I thought. *There is no need for the sun to shine in the sky, because my Mary lights up the Earth, brighter than any sun or moon or stars could ever be.* Her golden hair bounced slightly from side to side as she walked, her rosy cheeks could be seen from a mile, she was the sun, the rainbow all in one.

She reached her locker and began to look for the key. As she fumbled around in her pocket to find it, I took several slow steps in her direction, still hiding behind the daily news. When she finally opened the metal door, her eyes grew wide, and she gasped. She grabbed the rose and pendant. When she opened the locket and saw the photo, one she had given to me the day before she'd left Baghdad, she turned on her heels and began to look up and down the hallway. She seemed pale and confused, and I feared she might faint.

I was about twenty feet away, so I hurried toward her. "Hi, Mary," I said with a smile.

She said nothing, but she offered me a greeting that I would never forget: tears of joy, followed by a smile, followed by a warm embrace.

I quickly remembered we weren't alone, as there were still four or five students in the hallway. Our happy reunion had only taken seconds, and I hoped no one had seen us. "Meet me near the tennis courts in five minutes," I whispered, happy that Pauline had informed me that Mary had a forty-five minute break between classes.

At the tennis courts, we sat and talked, and I don't think I even blinked, as I couldn't bear to take my eyes off of her. Mary was happier than I'd ever seen her, and I could think of no words to describe the smile she continuously wore, just as there were no words to do justice to the absolute happiness I felt being near her again.

She told me every detail about her trip back to the UK and what had happened since, from the moment she left to Baghdad. "Life has been unbearable without you, Ali," she said. "I haven't been able to sleep, eat, or think straight. I've been miserable, feeling hopeless. Naseema has been so worried about me. She threw me a small party and invited all the neighbors, hoping to cheer me up, but that didn't help."

"It wasn't good to see all of your friends?" I asked.

"The only person I wanted to see was you," she admitted sheepishly, then looked out across the tennis courts. "Miss Naseema convinced me to come here, to Whitelands, to take some English literature courses. It has helped a little, but not really." she said and smiled back at me. "I've been in England this whole time physically, but my soul was left behind in Baghdad," she said. "Now that you're here, I have my soul back, and I can smile again." After she told me about her painful experiences, she asked how I managed to find her.

I told her all about my journey, starting with my visit to Mr. Radhi's house. "He helped me figure out where your family lives, and he also helped me fill out the paperwork. From there, I took a bus to Beirut and a plane to London. I arrived yesterday and did a little sightseeing, and this morning, I went to speak with Naseema."

"You did?" she asked, surprised. "Tell me more, Ali. Tell me everything."

She wanted every detail, including what I ate, drank, and wore along the way, and I was happy to fill her in. It seemed that Mary was coming back to life more and more with every word I spoke.

Those glorious forty-five minutes of conversation flew by in a heartbeat. Mary considered skipping to miss her next class so we could continue talking, but I encouraged her to follow her normal schedule. "Well, I usually go to a nearby park after class, to wait for James. It's a nice place for a walk and to do some thinking. It's only a ten-minute walk from here, so we can meet there when my class is over."

I agreed, and Mary gathered her books and hurried off to class.

After her class was over, she met me in the park, and we spent an hour there, just talking, holding hands, and walking beside the beautiful blue lake; even though the sky was gray, the rain had stopped, and I was glad for that—though I would have walked through a hurricane or a tsunami to be with Mary.

"I have to go back in a week," I told her. "Things have calmed down a little in Baghdad, but I still feel something is wrong."

"Well, all of my classes will be finished during the last week of January. There's no one to stop me from returning to Baghdad, Ali. Seeing you again has given me all the energy and desire I need to finish my studies here, and then I'll go back to where I belong—with you. Now that we've got Naseema on our side, it will be easier to convince my father."

For the next two days, we met at the park after her classes. James always gave me a ride there, and we asked him to pick her up an hour later than usual. On her last day of school before the Christmas holiday, we walked and walked all over the place. We carved our names in the bark of several trees, chased each other like children, and skipped stones in the lake.

By sheer luck, we happened upon a beautiful white wooden gazebo in a long-forgotten corner of the park. It had glass windows from the floor to the ceiling, and the architecture was stunning. It seemed abandoned, and we simply had to peek inside it. The handle on the door was quite rusty, but it wasn't locked, so we opened it and sat down inside. Strangely, the little structure felt like a home of our own. Inside it, we were alone—just my Mary and me—and no one could judge us by race, color, religion, or nationality. It was just Ali and Mary in that beautiful place, away from the cruel and narrow-minded of the world, at least for the few hours we spent there. Those were beautiful times, maybe the only two days we really felt free to show our emotions in public, and when time came for James to pick her up, we shared a long kiss goodbye.

The next day, Miss Naseema and Mary came to London to do some Christmas shopping at one of the stores. They were planning a small holiday gathering for some of their close relatives and friends, around twenty people, and I'd been invited. At first, I'd hesitated to accept, as I feared that word might reach the general and even Charles that I was in England; I feared their interference would have a negative effect on everything, but Mary assured me that neither her father nor Charles had spoken to the party guests in nearly a year, and they wouldn't see them for at least eight months. "By then," she said, "no one will even remember you were here— except me." As an extra precaution, we agreed that Mary and Miss Naseema would introduce me by another name, as Mary's Arabic teacher from Baghdad, a perfect cover story since she had done rather well picking the language up.

At nine in the morning, I met them at the store. An hour later, Miss Naseema told us, "You two go on and enjoy yourselves. I will be in this store for at least three more hours, and I'll find you when I'm finished."

Elated, we took off like schoolchildren being let out for recess. We walked for several blocks and came upon a cinema. It had always been a fantasy of ours to see a movie together. There were beautiful theaters in Baghdad, but they were always attended by the elite, and a foreigner on the arm of an Iraqi would have raised too many suspicious eyebrows. When we saw that *The King and I* was playing, a film starring the debonair Yul Brynner and the beautiful Deborah Kerr, we bought our tickets without a second thought and went inside. We loved the movie, held hands all time, and exchanged looks and smiles in the dark. We could very much relate with the leading man and his lady; like us, they were very much in love but were from two different worlds.

Having fulfilled one of the things on our wish list, we cheerfully made our way back to the department store. We still had around a half-hour to spend together, so we decided to have some tea at the next café we came upon.

The day before, Mary had told me she had a small surprise for me, and right after we sat down and ordered our tea and biscuits, she took out a little book, like one someone would use to store a postage stamp collection. She placed it on the table in front of me and asked me to open it.

As soon as I opened the cover and flipped through the pages, I knew that Mary loved me more than anyone in the world, and I suddenly didn't care what anyone had to say about us. I move closer to kiss her lips passionately, then kissed her soft, dainty hand. Inside the book were all the roses I'd thrown on her balcony back in Iraq, carefully dried and preserved and mounted on the pages, with an inscription beneath each indicating the date she'd received them. On the first page, there was a single rose next to a hand-drawn heart, with no date beneath it; it was the first rose I'd given her the day I showed her their new garden in Baghdad. Mary told me she slept with the book under her pillow, and when she said that, I wished the world would stop for eternity just so I'd have enough time to tell Mary again and again and again how much I loved her.

When we finally met up with Miss Naseema again, I invited her and Mary to lunch and indicated that I would also enjoy James's company. They had all been so kind to me, so accepting of me, and I wanted to show them my appreciation.

Lambeth was nice, there was a small restaurant near my bed-and-breakfast, and I'd already visited it once and had enjoyed the traditional English food. Even better than the cuisine was the flowers growing all about; it felt like eating lunch in the middle of a flourishing garden, surrounded by every color imaginable.

They accepted my invitation, and we all enjoyed a nice lunch and a lot of laughs. After lunch, I waved goodbye to my British friends, and they hurried home to prepare for the Christmas party the next day.

At that festive gathering, I was introduced as Omar, Mary's Arabic teacher. As the story went, I was in England on a four-day visit with an Iraqi delegation invited by some English-Arab organization.

Apart from the beautifully decorated ten-foot Christmas tree, the elegantly prepared living room we sat in, and the delicious food prepared, it wasn't really a night to remember in England—at least not how I had expected it would be.

Like many times before, Mary and I were slapped in the face with the harsh reality of our different worlds. I was blatantly insulted on two occasions by one of the guests. Right after dinner, one of the Thompsons' neighbors, asked, "Aren't you simply ecstatic being here, Omar, in real civilization, rather than that dreadful, dry, sticky desert you come from, where everything reeks of camel dung and is covered with sand and grit?" I attempted to ignore the remark and avoid conversation with him, but he continued talking, comparing the "amazingly convenient modern transportation systems of Britain" to the "four-legged, furry, slow-going animals" we all supposedly relied on to get around. "Tell me, Omar, what is it like to travel by bus and car and airplane rather than horse or camel or whatever other smelly creatures you have to ride back home?"

I responded in a very calm, dignified, mature manner, using far fewer and far kinder words than I secretly wanted to. "We have cars in Baghdad," I said. "As a matter of fact, I have two." I then kindly and intelligently reminded him that Arabs had invented the wheel, and when most of the human beings in the world were still living in caves, we had palaces. Careful not to sound too sarcastic, I said, "If you have any doubt about that, sir, perhaps you should consult the history books written by your own British historians, or maybe you can pay a visit to your British Museum, which finds Arab and Middle East history interesting and significant enough to boast its treasures to your people here."

My reply stunned the arrogant man into silence, and I excused myself and left the place before he could even come up with a snarky reply.

Mary followed me and just laughed. "I love your confidence, Ali. I think by now we are both immune to the cruel and twisted things nosy, condescending fools have to say, aren't we?" She laughed again and took my hand. "Ali, you were right when you told me at your party that it will be you and I against the world, but I don't care anymore I love you, my Iraqi prince, and we will always be together. I must admit that I somewhat enjoy the scandal of it all, as it brings some intrigue to our relationship when everyone is jealous and things are a bit...edgy."

I smiled at her, noticing a naughty gleam in her eye. "Miss Mary Thompson, are you suggesting that you, the daughter of a British general, have a bit of a rebellious streak behind those emerald-green eyes of yours?"

"I do in fact, Ali," she said, "and I know you love me for it." She laughed again, then looked back up at me. "You needn't put up with that self-aggrandizing neighbor of ours any longer. James will gladly take you back to Lambeth now. I suggest you get some rest and clear your head, because we still have a couple of days left to enjoy each other here...and I can't wait to be back in Baghdad after that," she said.

We shared another unforgettable kiss on her beautiful terrace, beneath the silvery light of a half-moon, with the cool, gentle breeze of a British December making us appreciate one another's warm embrace all the more.

At the airport, two days later, we said our goodbyes and promised each other that it would be our last cruel departure from one another. I was so glad I'd made the brave trip to England. Once again, my Mary was full of life, happy, confident, and determined to finish her courses so she could reunite with me in my beloved homeland.

I enjoyed my time in Britain, and it was a learning experience, but I knew I could not stay there forever. I would never quite fit in, not even with the proper hat, and while most people I'd met had been kind and hospitable, there were still many who treated me like a lower life form. In Britain, I learned that class was not always exhibited by those perceived to be at its peak.

Around forty-eight hours later, I was back in Baghdad. I sat down with my workers at the nursery to see how business had been while I was away. I also gave each of them a small souvenir from my trip, and we talked about the things I'd seen in England and some new ideas and future plans that had been inspired by my trip.

I then went to Mustafa's favorite café, and I was glad to see him there. I sat down to have tea with my cousin, excited to tell him about my own world travels.

"Ali," he said, before I could tell him about my trip, "I have some news."

"Go on," I said, a bit concerned.

"I have decided to stop traveling and to open my own gold and jewelry shop right here in Baghdad. What do you think of that, cousin?"

The decision made me happy, as I loved my cousin and often worried about him when he was gone for months on end. The fact that he would be in Baghdad all the time excited me, as he was my best friend as well as my blood.

"So...tell me about your trip to England," he said.

Realizing that many people would be interested in my tale, and not wanting to repeat it over and over again, I replied, "Finish your tea and come with me to Mr. Radhi's house. I've got lot to tell all of you, including a little exciting news of my own."

A short while later, I was sitting with Mustafa, Mr. Radhi, and Madam Laila at their house. I began by thanking Mr. Radhi for all his help with the trip arrangements and for all the great tips and advice he'd given me. Then I went into all the details about what had happened.

My beloved audience listened carefully to every word I said, and Mustafa was visibly angry when I told him about the rude teenagers on the train, the way some of the college students had glared at me, and the disgustingly condescending neighbor at the Christmas party. When I saw that the atmosphere was growing a bit tense in light of the awful moments I'd experienced amidst my bliss with Mary, I decided to stop talking about my trip and asked, "What is new here? What has been going on in Baghdad?"

Mr. Radhi informed me, "Not much has changed in the last week, Ali. There've been a few minor shifts in parliament, new people coming in and old ones going out, as usual," he said, trying to sound nonchalant, but something in his tone suggested otherwise.

*What's really cooking in Baghdad?* I wondered. *Is trouble brewing once again...or still?* Nevertheless, I could tell Mr. Radhi didn't feel like talking about it or elaborating, so I didn't push the issue. I was too busy enjoying the afterglow from my time with Mary to taint my good mood with political unrest, doom, and gloom anyway.

After dinner, while we were having tea, I told them my decision. "I've had enough of this sneaking around and being afraid to be in love," I said. "I know you have all warned me of the dangers, but I am going to marry Miss Mary Thompson. It is only a matter of time. She will be back in February, and a month or two after that, I will take that step. I'm not sure of all the details of the proposal and how we will arrange the wedding, but I refuse to play hide-and-seek anymore. I love her, and she loves me, and we have chosen to be together, no matter what my society or hers has to say about it."

Madam Laila was the first to hug me and congratulate me, and Mr. Radhi and Mustafa assured me that they both had my back. With Mary, Miss Naseema, my dear cousin, and my mentors by my side, I knew my future would eventually come together just as I hoped.

Winter was in its last weeks when Mary finally arrived. It was not as much of a hassle to get in to see her, since Miss Naseema knew our secrets and supported our relationship. Mr. Dalton still had no idea, but he was a professional who tried not to interfere in the personal lives of those he worked for. Besides that, Mr. Dalton seemed to like me, so he gave me no trouble at all.

Mary and I usually met at the markets or my nursery, and once a week, we visited the Alwiyah club, a social club established by the British Embassy in 1924.

Whenever we met there for tea, Miss Naseema accompanied us, since the place was attended by many British military personnel, and we didn't want to be seen there alone.

April 23 was like any other Tuesday, or so it seemed, though I later realized it would turn out to be the craziest day of my life. Everything happened so fast. I met Miss Naseema and Mary at the Alwiyah, and after we had lunch and tea, we took a short walk in the garden. Then, for a few minutes, Naseema gave us some time alone.

I was back at the nursery around three p.m. Two hours later, three gentlemen showed up at my gate, two Iraqi policemen and a British military man. They asked me to accompany them to the police station for questioning.

I knew at once that it wasn't a normal situation. If it had only been the Iraqis, I wouldn't have been so worried, but the presence of the British soldier meant there was more to it than a simple inquisition about a local or business matter. I told one of my workers to find Mustafa and tell him what had happened, and I sent my other worker to run and fetch Mr. Radhi at once. It was all I could think to do at the time, but in hindsight, I realize I should have done more, like run away myself. I took some belongings from one of the drawers and left with the men, unaware that it would be the last time I ever laid eyes on my nursery.

I was taken to the police station in al Risafah, and they kept me completely in the dark and gave me no clue as to what was going on. I was held in a small interrogation room, nearly empty except for a well-worn wooden table, an ashtray, two chairs, and a small, circular window that was too high for me to see through.

After I sat there for forty-five minutes, worrying about my fate and wondering what I'd done, the British soldier returned. Without offering me an introduction or any explanation whatsoever, he got straight to the point. "We need answers right now," he demanded. "What is your relationship with Dr. Kamal? What do you know about him?"

I was taken aback by the questions, but as I thought about it, I realized that my acquaintance with Dr. Kamal, a known communist, might be the source of my trouble. I told him what I knew and when I'd last seen the doctor.

The answer was not thorough enough for him, and he quickly turned red in the face with anger. He began speaking more aggressively, demanding that I tell him of Dr. Kamal's whereabouts.

"I-I have no idea where he is," I stuttered.

At that point, he began to shout and banged his fists on the rickety old table, cursing at me and threatening, "You'd better tell me the truth, or else you are going to be in deep trouble." He went on and on and eventually blurted out, "Ali, where are you hiding the doctor? Tell me now!"

At that point, I realized how serious the situation was. I nervously repeated to him several times, "I am not keeping him anywhere. I don't know where he is. I know nothing!"

Tired of my unhelpful answers, he stopped asking me questions and began making blatant accusations. "We know the doctor is a communist, Ali, and we also know you are part of his cell. We know you have been meeting with that wicked troublemaker. You are an accomplice, a party to their crimes, and justice will be served on you, just as it will be on them," he said, then got up to leave.

After two hours of questioning, threats, and accusations, I was left alone for another hour. It may have been an attempt to break me psychologically on their part, but I needed that time to clear my head and think. I kept going through the scenarios, asking myself questions, wondering how I'd gotten mixed up in that political nightmare when politics were usually the furthest thing from my mind. *Why me?* I wondered *And why now?* The answers to those questions would come later, once the whole ugly tapestry of lies was woven together.

It became dark before anyone came to see me again. Major Amin, a middle-aged man who was the head of the station, asked if I was doing okay and if I'd been treated well. "My wife has mentioned your handiwork," he said. "She says you are a magician when it comes to gardening and landscape design, and from what one of my officers tells me, you are a peaceful man with a smile on his face. He's often seen you at the local cafés."

I wasn't sure whether or not to feel relieved and complimented, because it gave me an eerie feeling to know that people had been talking about me and watching me when I was unaware of it.

The major moved his chair closer to mine and sat down beside me. He seemed to be an honest, helpful man, and he calmly fanned through my file and said, "Ali, this doesn't make sense. There are not even any witnesses. The truth is, I am unaware of any charges being pressed against you, and I am not sure why you are here."

"In that case, sir, am I free to go?" I mumbled hopefully.

He held his hand up, as if to tell me he wasn't done talking. "Around four p.m. today, I received a letter from the British military demanding that you be brought in for questioning. I am sorry if we have frightened or inconvenienced you, but we must follow protocol and direct orders, Ali. I hope you understand." Major Amin then went through a series of routine questions. "Are you connected with any political parties? Have you been engaged in any activity that might be deemed illegal or suspicious?"

"No," I answered truthfully. "I only run my business. I don't go to any political gatherings, and none of my friends are involved with it either. In fact, I try to distance myself from politics altogether, because it's a grim topic that causes people to fight, and I don't like to talk about it."

The major thought about my answer for a few moments. "Mm-hmm," he said, scratching his chin, and it seemed like he believed me. "Just wait here for a while, Ali, and I'm hoping we can get this all cleared up and get you out of here by nine." Then, he picked up the file and walked out of the room, locking the door behind him.

I was certain the major believed me, especially since I'd told him the truth. As I sat there, I wondered if that nasty Charles, in a jealous and vengeful rage, had instigated the whole thing to get back at me, but I dismissed that from my mind and tried to wait patiently for them to clear my record so I could go home. As I sat, I tried to concentrate on Mary, which always helped me to pass the time.

Only twenty minutes later, Major Amin returned. This time, he looked a bit different, as if he'd seen a ghost. I could sense that he knew something, and whatever it was, the news wasn't good.

"Ali," he said, "we have just received notification from the British military that you are to be transferred first thing in the morning to Al Habbaniya for further investigation. Your place of business will be closed until further notice, pending these investigations."

"What!?" I said in disbelief, beginning to panic. "But I—"

Again, the major held up his hand to silence me. "Witnesses have come forward to testify and provide details. These testimonies mention your direct involvement with Dr. Kamal, a man believed to be behind several skirmishes and incidents of political unrest in

Baghdad and elsewhere. The British have been searching for the suspected communist for weeks now, as he is being blamed for an incident that resulted in several casualties of their soldiers a few weeks ago. Ali, I know what you told me, but these new reports clearly indicate that you were part of all that, and you are now considered a threat to the national security of this country and all of Britain."

"Who are these witnesses?" I asked, now pounding my own fist on the table, though not with nearly the brute force that the British soldier had used; his hands had been hardened by war, while mine were still soft from rose petals and soil. "None of this makes any sense, Major," I complained.

"The witnesses are respectable men, high-ranking military officers, General Thompson and Lieutenant Charles. They are men of great reputation among the British military ranks, and their testimonies carry a lot of weight. They claim they have seen you meeting with Dr. Kamal several times. A café owner also validates their story, as he recalls seeing you there with Dr. Kamal and overhearing talk about some sort of inevitable change in the works among the Iraqi people."

My worst suspicions had come to fruition, and I worried that all of this was because of my closeness with Mary. I knew Charles had some very outspoken animosity against me, but I had never realized the general felt the same way. I had bumped into Dr. Kamal at that café, quite by accident, and there had been talk of the political unrest in Iraq—talk I quickly wanted to escape. But that had been so long ago, and I couldn't figure out why they had waited so long to charge me. There was something more to the story, something missing, and that only worried me more.

I could tell that Major Amin was an understanding man, and I had to prove my innocence to him. I told him everything I knew about Dr. Kamal, which wasn't much, and I admitted to meeting him a few times and even inviting him to my party, along with many other elite personalities in Baghdad.

Major Amin continued to scribble notes in the file. "Are there any personal issues between you and Dr. Kamal, or perhaps the general, the lieutenant, or the café owner has something against you?" he asked.

That time, I declined to reply. Regardless of what they did to me, I refused to drag Mary's name into it.

The major hadn't only been born yesterday, and he had seen and heard it all in his time. He had sat down and spoken with people from all walks of society during his illustrious twenty-eight year military career. He had investigated countless cases and people and had interrogated hundreds, from criminals to serious political leaders to psychopaths and killers to those who were completely innocent. He was an expert at sensing things about people, at reading them, and I could tell from the start that deep down, he knew I was innocent.

Finally, he closed his notebook and said, "Ali, tell me, what is this personal matter between you and our two stellar witnesses."

Again, I refused to answer. I didn't want to drag Mary into the mess. It was my problem, and I had to solve it. "I have nothing more to say," I said, "other than that I am innocent."

He smiled. "That's all the answer I need," he said. He wanted to help me and didn't like being on the wrong side of honesty and justice, and he wasn't afraid to fight the system when he knew they were doing wrong. "Think this all over and call me if you have anything more to tell me. I wish you the best of luck, Ali," he said before he left the room. Over his shoulder, just before he stepped out the door, he hollered, "You have a visitor. I'll send him in."

Mustafa, my faithful cousin, hurried into the room in a huff. I could sense fear and rage glistening in his eyes. Contrary to his usually laidback nature, he was in a hurry and spoke faster than I had ever heard him talk before, giving me the details of what had happened. "That fiend Charles hasn't been in Al Habaniyah like we thought. He was lurking around in the shadows at the Alwiyah when you were there with Naseema and Mary, Ali, spying on you. When he saw you and Mary go on a walk, holding hands, he went crazy. In a jealous rage, he called General Thompson, and within an hour after Mary left the club, they confronted her about it."

I couldn't imagine what poor Mary must have gone through, and I was grateful that Mustafa spared me the details.

"Major Amin is a good person, Ali. Just tell him about Mary. That will save your neck."

141

"No!" I yelled. Then, realizing someone might be listening, I leaned over and whispered to my cousin, "I will not bring her into this."

"Ali, if you do not tell the major, I will. You can hate me forever, but he must know the truth about the two of you. It's for your own good."

"Not only will I hate you, Mustafa," I said, snarling at him like an angry animal, "but I will kill you if you utter a word of it to anyone. I do not want Mary to be burned with more trouble than she is already in."

Mustafa smirked. "Fine. Kill me, Ali...but you can't kill everyone who knows, can you?" With that, he got up and left.

Five minutes later, the major opened the door. "Ali, my questions have been answered, and I know the allegations against you are false. You are free to go for now, and I will take care of everything the next morning."

I graciously thanked him and left. I was ready to murder Mustafa to pay him back for his loose tongue, but when I saw Mary in the car with Mr. Radhi, Madam Laila, and Mustafa, I was speechless. I was even more stunned by the sight of the bruise on Mary's soft cheek, a purple and yellowing blemish on that flawless canvas.

Before I could say a thing, Mr. Radhi explained, "She's fine, Ali. Do not worry. Your Mary is a strong lady, strong enough to be your wife by tomorrow."

With tears in her eyes, Mary kissed me, and so did Madam Laila. Mary told me, "Daddy was furious when he heard about us, and he attacked me, Ali! He was hitting me, and Charles was shouting like a madman. I swear, it looked as if his eyes were on fire. If it hadn't been for my dear Naseema and that brave Mr. Dalton, I don't know what would have happened. Mr. Dalton couldn't stand seeing anyone lay a hand on me, not even my brute of a father."

I was happy to hear that Mr. Dalton had helped rescue Mary. I'd always admired the man, and I knew he would stand up for her when it was necessary. "How did you get away, my love?" I asked, gently caressing the cheek that wasn't bruised and growing furious that they had dared to make a mark on her.

"Mr. Dalton and Naseema got me away from them and then secretly gave me a ride to Mr. Radhi's house so he could help me find you."

We all listened carefully while Mr. Radhi told us of his brilliant plan. "You two should spend the night at my house. Tomorrow morning, just before eight a.m., we will take you to the courthouse so you can be married. I have already spoken with one of the judges, a friend of mine, and Mr. Dalton and Naseema will meet us there."

Miss Naseema was Mary's guardian and could legally serve as a credible witness for the marriage, and Mr. Dalton was willing to sign as a witness as well, this will be for our own records. My friend, the judge will bury the legal papers, and not a soul can find out. By the time the British military arrived to transport me from the station, we'd already be married and would be on our way to Samarra. From there, we would take the bus to Sulaymaniyah, where we would stay with Kaka Hawazin, an old man Mr. Radhi trusted with his life. Major Amin had promised Mr. Radhi that he would delay the British transport as long as possible. "That's my job," he said. "Just leave it to me, and I'll take care of it. If I have anything to say about it, they will not get their conniving hands on Ali and his bride."

Much to our delight and relief, all went according to plan, and by one p.m. the next day, I was on the bus with Mary, my wife. The only belongings we had in our possession were one bag for each of us, our marriage certificate, Kaka Hawazin's address, and a letter from Mr. Radhi addressed to the man.

Halfway through our journey, I was staring at the window as cities and villages passed by and the landscape began to change. Mary was sound asleep, resting her head on my shoulder. She had cried a lot, and her goodbyes to Miss Naseema and Mr. Dalton were painful. She was also worried that our new life on the run would be difficult, but she assured me that most of her tears were tears of joy because she'd be spending that life with me. Whether from pain or joy, the tears had left her eyes red and tired, and I was glad to know she was getting some much-needed rest.

I, on the other hand, couldn't possibly sleep. My mind continued to spin and my stomach churned a bit as I pondered how the situation would affect those I knew. I wondered how the general, Charles, and the British would react to me fleeing and whisking Mary away with me. For all intents and purposes, I was a criminal, a fugitive. I thought about Mustafa, my uncle, my family, and the beautiful years I'd spent in Baghdad. I smiled when the wise and helpful Mr. Radhi and the lovely and kind Madam Laila crossed my mind. Then I thought of Baghdad, the city I'd loved from the first time I set my eyes on it as a child. I remembered my nursery in vivid detail, the talk of the city, and I wondered, *Will I ever see it again?*

We reached Sulaymaniyah around seven p.m., a region in the northeastern part of Iraq, populated by proud Kurds. Historically, the Kurds had tried several times to declare their independence, most notably under the leadership of Sheikh Mahmud Barzinji, the king of Kurdistan in the late 1910s and early 1920s. Barzinji ultimately failed, and he accepted the fate and signed a peace treaty declaring Sulaymaniyah part of Iraq in 1932. Sulaymaniyah was a land of magnificent, mountainous landscapes, waterfalls, and green, plush grass, trees, and foliage as far as the eyes could see.

After transferring to two more buses and walking for twenty minutes, we reached Kaka Hawazin's house; it is a known custom that "Kaka" was the first name of nearly every Kurdish man, and it meant something similar to mister or sir.

His house was isolated, situated on a small hill, two miles from his nearest neighbor. It was dark when we arrived, but we could still tell that his place was lovely, overlooking the partly lit city center. The house itself was very simple, a brick and mud dwelling with one floor, forty meters long and ten meters wide, in the shape of a rectangle. The narrow home had four windows, one on each end and two big ones in the middle. Some olive trees were growing near the entrance, flanked by one palm tree and an orange tree.

I knocked on the door several times before I saw movement through the middle window and heard the footsteps of someone approaching.

A short man, presumably in his late forties or early fifties, opened the door. He had very white skin that almost glowed in contrast to his black hair. His face was round, and he had big blue eyes and very thick eyebrows that connected above the bridge of his nose. As far as his physique, while he wasn't of tall stature, he was well built, with very broad shoulders. He smiled at us and greeted us in Kurdish.

I handed Mr. Radhi's letter to him.

He stood in the doorway and read it, then pulled me into a hug. "Any son of Mr. Radhi's is a son of mine," he said in a language that I could understand. He then welcomed us in and called for his wife. When she scurried into the room, he said, "Ready Serwan's room. We have guests."

Serwan, his only son, had died several years earlier, leaving behind a widow and an infant. The baby, a beautiful little girl named Sara, was now three years old, as we learned when Kaka Hawazin sat down with us and introduced us to his small family. "This is my wife, Fatema Khan, and my daughter-in-law, Sayran," he said, "and from this day on, we are your family."

When he pulled me aside from the women and asked me what had happened back in Baghdad, I told him everything. The man was willing to give me, a fugitive from the crooked law, safe harbor, and for bearing such a risk, he deserved to know the truth. Besides that, Mr. Radhi trusted him, and that meant a lot.

He was very calm and didn't show any signs of fear, even when I mentioned that the British military was probably after me. "Just lie low for a while," he said. "You and your beautiful bride will be safe and comfortable here, with us, and you needn't go anywhere until everything calms down. I'll keep my eyes and ears open for news when I am in town."

He informed me that he was into the livestock business, and he owned over a hundred cattle, forty goats, eleven cows, and dozens of chickens. He'd done well for himself, and his worth continued to increase, enabling him to provide for his family. He'd been raising livestock for nearly twelve years, since Mr. Radhi's father, his former employer, had passed away. Prior to that, Kaka Hawazin had worked for Mr. Radhi's family all his life. When Mr. Radhi found out that Kaka Hawazin desired to marry and work for himself, he gave him some money to start a new life with his bride, and Kaka Hawazin decided to return to Sulaymaniyah, his home.

When our room was arranged, Kaka Hawazin left us to rest after our long trip, but he mentioned that I should wake up early, because there was plenty of work to do. He hoped the work with the animals would help me take my mind off my troubles, and I didn't mind helping him. It was the least I could do, and it allowed me to feel useful once again.

Our room was small but very beautiful, and the blankets were soft and colorful; the family was simple and were not the wealthiest of people, but they had taste. Mary and I turned off the lamp and opened the windows. We could see millions of stars, more than we'd ever seen before, and it was a beautiful setting for our first night as a married couple. We reminisced about how we'd first met and laughed about all the days that had passed since then. We recalled the special times we'd spent in Baghdad and London, and we comforted each other when our hearts ached for the people we had to leave behind in order for us to be together. We were thankful to be married at last, even if it had not been the wedding we'd dreamt of, and when we began to kiss and made love for the first time, it was absolute bliss—a honeymoon under the stars, away from all the turmoil that had almost ripped us apart.

I woke up at seven a.m. and saw that Mary was still asleep, exhausted from the whirlwind of life-changing events of the past few days. I gave her a kiss on the cheek and was drawn to the kitchen by the enticing aroma of coffee brewing.

Kaka Hawazin's wife, Madam Fatema, didn't speak Arabic very well, but I understood her well enough, and her kindness cut through any language barrier. She poured me some coffee and gave me a sandwich, then told me that Hawazin was already outside.

"Thank you," I said, then quickly grabbed the cheese sandwich and joined him.

"Did you sleep well, young friend?" he asked.

"Yes."

"Good. Then you are well rested and will not be late to report to work again. From tomorrow on, Ali, work will start promptly at six thirty. We mustn't tarry in our slumber when the animals are hungry!"

Kaka spent the first hour explaining the work routine to me, then showed me my specific duties. He was very organized and repeated his instructions several times over so that I wouldn't miss anything important. While the work wasn't difficult, it was rather mundane and tiring. For several hours, I had to walk the cattle around a path, a rather long distance. I was used to walking and working early in the morning, and I'd been under the sun for long hours before; after all, I had been brought up on a farm. Still, while the responsibilities of agriculture and livestock were somewhat similar, there were some differences in the routine.

Around one p.m., we returned home, filthy and tired. We both took a quick bath to wash off the manure, sweat, and dirt, then joined the ladies for lunch.

Mary seemed to enjoy working in the kitchen, helping Madam Fatema prepare the various dishes. When she smiled, the whole room lit, and just seeing her so happy washed away all the sorrow and bitterness I felt from being forced out of Baghdad.

⁘⁛⁘

As much as we missed Baghdad, Kaka Hawazin had a beautiful home, a thriving business, and a loving family, and it didn't take long for Mary and for me to adapt to our new surroundings. They were helpful in everything and made sure we were comfortable and had everything we needed. We made it a point to learn a little Kurdish each day, and in time, I grew to love working with the livestock. My wife even learned to knit, with Sayran and Madam Fatema's patient teaching, and she was becoming a better cook by the day.

Weeks passed, and we never once left the property. The farthest we had dared to go together was for a walk down Kaka Hawazin's lane. I hadn't heard any news from Baghdad, and Kaka Hawazin hadn't heard any rumors or unusual talk, so that was somewhat of a comfort. I hoped that our enemies had, perhaps, forgotten about us or given up the chase.

During our fourth week there, just as Kaka and I were finishing our morning work for the day and were heading in for lunch, we heard voices. As we neared the house, they rang very familiar in my ears, and a well of joy sprang up in me. *Mr. Radhi and Mustafa are here!*

It was a delight and a relief to see them again, and we all enjoyed lunch together. After tea was served, the women left us to talk. The official news in Baghdad was that I had kidnapped a British general's daughter. As for what was being said by the common folk in the street and in the shops, rumors were running rampant. Some considered it as the greatest love story they'd ever heard and believed we'd followed our hearts and had left Iraq and were living somewhere in the UK. A few believed the accusations about me, that I'd kidnapped her. Some even believed the British had already caught me and that I was serving my sentence in a prison at the Al Habaniyah base.

Most considered me a victim of foul play spawned by jealousy, and they often clashed with the British authorities who were in Baghdad looking for me. Regardless of what people believed, I was the talk of Baghdad—and this time, it had nothing to do with gardening.

"When the British came to pick you up from the temporary prison," Mr. Radhi said, "Major Amin told them a fib, claiming you'd escaped during the night. The British troops were none too happy about that!" he exclaimed, then laughed heartily, rubbing his belly. "Around noon that same day, after Miss Naseema and Mr. Dalton were sure you were long gone and safe, they informed the general that Mary was missing. At that point, all hell broke loose, and the British went on high alert. Ali, you wouldn't believe all the chaos you caused for those first few days. Security was tight all around Baghdad, and it stretched to all the cities. Although the Iraqi police have their doubts that you kidnapped Mary, they have to comply with the British. No one knows exactly what to do, since a British general's daughter has never gone missing before in Iraq. You've caused quite a stir, my son."

"They dragged Mr. Radhi and me in for questioning," Mustafa said. "They only kept him there for a few hours, but they locked me in that room for several days, and when they couldn't force me to tell them anything, they finally let me go, but I think they've been following us." Mustafa sighed and shook his head. "Can you believe they even searched our family farm in

Diyala?" He went on to tell me that everyone whom I'd ever come in contact with had been taken in for questioning, from my workers at the nursery to the people I played dominos with at the café.

"The general and Charles tried to accuse Miss Naseema of helping you escape, but she put on a show like no other," Mr. Radhi said, grinning from ear to ear. "That lady is quite an actress. Never losing her straight face, she acted as if she was in shock about Mary and even pretended to faint several times. She publicly blamed the general for the loss of her beloved Mary and turned the tables on them with her manic shouting and crying."

They told me that my nursery had remained closed and had been heavily guarded at all times. "Most of your plants have died due to neglect, Ali," Mustafa said sadly, knowing that my gardens had been my pride and joy. "It is a horrible sight."

"You must be careful, Ali," Mr. Radhi cautioned. "The British believe you have fled the country, and they assume you are in Syria or Turkey by now, but you never know where eyes are watching, ears are listening, and tongues are blabbing," he said in a tone that reminded Ali of his father's voice from long ago.

"How are you and Mary doing?" my cousin asked. "Are you comfortable here, enjoying your life as newlyweds?"

I looked at Kaka Hawazin and smiled. "We're in very good hands, cousin, and Mary and I couldn't be happier. We still haven't decided on our next step, but we enjoy being in Sulaymaniyah—at least in this house. Sooner or later, we'll sort everything out and figure out where to go from here."

Mr. Radhi gave me a letter from Madam Laila, an emotional communication filled with encouragement and lovely words of wisdom. "Give her a kiss on the forehead for me when you get back," I said, and he agreed that he would.

We enjoyed the rest of the day together, sitting out in the fresh air and sipping delicious coffee Madam Fatema made for us. We talked and laughed over dinner, and everyone seemed so happy to be reunited.

"How are Naseema and Mr. Dalton? Well, I hope," Mary said, as she missed them a lot.

"They both seem to be doing rather well, in spite of your father's antics," Mr. Radhi told her.

"Good. Please tell my Naseema that I am very happy and safe in Ali's arms, and she needn't worry about me," she said with a tear in her eye, longing for her second mother.

Mustafa and Mr. Radhi left early the next day and promised that they'd be back soon. "Don't worry," Mr. Radhi said to my crying wife, who didn't like farewells at all. "This visit is just the first of many. You both have enough friends that you will never be lonely."

⁖⁖⁖

Days and days went by, and Mary and I thought our situation over very carefully. We knew Baghdad wasn't a feasible option, at least not for the foreseeable future, since I was a wanted man there. It would be

153

difficult and lonely to leave the country, since we'd both be strangers in some strange new world. We wanted to be around people and cultures we knew and understood. I didn't know how long we could safely remain at Kaka Hawazin's house, but it seemed like the best option for the time being, and we truly felt like he and his wife, daughter-in-law, and granddaughter were family. My only regret was that I didn't want to be a burden to them.

I had saved up some money during my years as a successful gardener in Baghdad, so one day, while we were sitting in his hallway, I told him, "Kaka, Mary and I would like to stay with you for a while, and I want to invest more than cattle-walking in your business, as a financial partner."

"Come outside with me," he said. After we walked outdoors, he grabbed the ladder that was lying next to the back door and asked me to climb on top of his house with him. When we reached the roof, he pointed out across the landscape. "Look at all that I have, Ali," he said, pointing at the rolling hills and herds of livestock. "If it wasn't for Mr. Radhi, I would have none of it. That man, my benefactor, considers you to be his son, and what I am providing for you and Mary pales in comparison to the generosity that Mr. Radhi and his father before him have shown to me. You are not indebted to me, Ali, for Mr. Radhi has paid any debt you could possibly owe a hundred times over. You are not a burden to me or my wife, and you are not obliged to invest your hard-earned money in my business. You are already a partner."

I thanked him for his kind words but told him I'd be much happier and more comfortable if he would let me offer some help. I insisted, and in the end, he told me to do whatever I needed to do to make me happy.

I bought a few cattle for myself and continued to work with the livestock in the mornings, while Mary busied herself with knitting and learning Kurdish, a very unique language indeed. In return, she taught English to the other women, both of whom proved to be quick learners.

My wife and I spent our evenings together, taking long walks deep into Kaka Hawazin's land, always hand in hand, enjoying the landscape, the sunsets, and the view of mountains in the horizon. What we enjoyed most was the endless blanket of stars, which we'd marveled over since our first night there. The velvety black cosmos seemed to sparkle with millions of them, and we gazed up at them and connected them with our minds in the shape of our dream home. We imagined a huge house, a home of our own, with balconies, trees, and flowers. We imagined people dancing in our gardens, all of them happy for us and enjoying the love we shared and the fruits of our labors. The cruel world had taken much from us, but it couldn't take away the stars, our love, or our fantasies of a brighter future.

We were isolated from society, from the whole world, in fact, and we hadn't left Kaka's property in over two months, but we were happy, and we had each other.

Still, something seemed to be missing, and as I watched Mary play with little Sara, Kaka Hawazin's beautiful granddaughter, chasing after the child and dressing her up, I realized what that one thing was: We needed to make a baby, a child of our own that would be the embodiment of our love.

⁘

It had been 96 days, 2,304 hours, since Mary and I had first knocked on Kaka Hawazin's door, and neither of us had left his two-acre premises since. All that changed one day when Kaka Hawazin said, "Things are settling down, I think, and if you are very, very careful, I think you can safely visit the city now."

He had already started telling people that some of his friends from southern Iraq had come to live with them, and he referred to me, his new partner, as Omar, the same name Mary and Miss Naseema had chosen for me as a bluff during my visit to the UK. He advised Mary to change her looks, and we agreed that dying her hair black would be the safest thing to do; with the abaya, she wouldn't be recognized. As for me, the beard I'd grown over the past month was more than enough.

"Go only to crowded places," Kaka advised. "With your new looks and your fair command of the common language, you will blend into the horde."

Our first visit to the city felt like our first date, as it had been so long since we'd been out in civilization. Our trip to the old market The Souq on that sunny afternoon was an exciting experience, albeit a bit anxious, as with every step we took, we were darting our

156

eyes about, looking right and left and over our shoulders, terrified that we might inadvertently run into police, military men, spies, or gossipers. Luckily for us, there weren't very many police officers in that part of the country, and it was partly ruled by the Kurds themselves. Nevertheless, the fear lingered and probably would for the rest of our lives.

Just after the afternoon prayer, Kaka Hawazin dropped us off at a market in the center of the city. It was a busy place, just like the markets in Baghdad, and it reminded us of the clothing and fabric shop where we'd rendezvoused so many times back home.

The love of colored fabric from the Kurds outnumbered the Arabs in Baghdad, and red was a very popular color. The women bargained and haggled over the price of red silk, red dresses, and all sorts of garments in every shade of crimson, maroon, and burgundy. Most of the bargaining words we understood, though we had to hear some more than once before we got the gist of it. Like all the other women, Mary joined the hunt for a perfect red dress that would look stunning on her. She was a social creature by nature and was thrilled to be around people again, as I was. Although our appearances and names were false, we were happy to join in with the crowd, and we began to feel like our old selves again.

While I had very much surprised her with my visit to her university so long ago, Mary was truly the master of surprises. At precisely the right moment, while we were busy in one of the shops, she asked me to measure the red silk she intended to buy. She wrapped it around herself and ask, "What do you think, Ali?"

"It is a beautiful color on you and a perfect fit," I said.

"Hmm," she said, tapping her chin with her finger and looking down at her belly. "Now that I think about it, Ali," she whispered in my ear, "I think I'll need a bit more fabric."

"Why?" I asked, confused, because it seemed more than ample to cover her thin frame.

"Because our baby will need room in my dress too," she said. When I still didn't understand and looked at her in confusion, she rolled her eyes and clarified, "Ali, I think I'm pregnant!"

In the past, many of my friends had told me how amazing it was the first time they heard that they were going to be a father, and I finally understood their glee. *Pregnant*? It was astonishing how that one simple word could make me feel so much love for my wife and for the child that was already growing inside of her. In an instant, it was as if everything I loved had become even more lovable, something I never thought possible. I adored Mary with all my heart and soul, but at that moment, my heart soared to heights I never thought existed, as if my love had no limits at all. My emotions could not be described with the mouth or written down, because there simply were no words. As I think about it now, writing this, I still feel a spiritual lift, and a whole year later, I feel as if I'm flying all over again. I hugged her so

tightly and instantly begged her to take care of herself
and demanded that she rest from that moment on.

·:˝·:˝

I was very happy that Mary was in Madam
Fatema's and Sayran's gentle, capable, caring hands.
They were so kind to her and treated her like a queen,
and there wasn't a thing she needed that wasn't
provided; she never had to ask twice.

I asked Kaka Hawazin to send our exciting news
to Baghdad, but I didn't want Mary to know that I had
sent word. Mary received a surprise of her own when
Madam Laila, Mr. Dalton, and her beloved Miss Naseema
showed up for an unexpected visit. Fortunately, the letter
I'd sent with one of Kaka Hawazin's friends to Madam
Laila in Baghdad had arrived safely, and since the general
was back in the UK for a fortnight, Naseema and Mr.
Dalton couldn't pass up the opportunity to visit their
long-missed Mary.

The few days they spent with us had to be some
of the happiest. I had missed Madam Laila, and I enjoyed
talking to her in the star-lit evenings. She had always
been encouraging to me, like a second mother, and I felt
it was a blessing from God that she and Mr. Radhi had
stepped into my life, one of the greatest couples on
Earth. Like my own parents would have been had they
survived, those two were the rock I depended on.

Mary spent many hours sitting outside with Miss
Naseema. She always asked about her father, for even
though he had hurt her physically and in her heart, he
was her father, her daddy, and she loved him

nonetheless. I didn't believe he deserved her love, but that was not for me to say.

※

Months passed, and everything was calm and sweet for us. We went out once a week and often had picnics in the nice weather or visited the markets when we felt like shopping or being social. The Kurds were friendly people.

Our visitors from Baghdad came often and always stayed for a few days. It was so good to see Mr. Radhi, Madam Laila, Mustafa, and Miss Naseema. My nursery had been seized, and no one was permitted to buy it or live in it. Both Mustafa and my poor old uncle had been taken in several times for questioning, though it never did any good, because neither of them would give me away.

Charles was still up to no good, with revenge still blackening his heart and raging in his mind. He ran into Mr. Radhi one day and said, "When I find Ali, which I will one day, I will not wait for the law to decide his fate. He has stolen Mary away from me and her father, and I will execute him myself for that."

The general, on the other hand, had been rather quiet and invisible, though Mr. Radhi did bump into him at a gathering. "I have never seen such a sad, defeated-looking man," Radhi told me. "He has aged so much since I last saw him, as if every passing day has been a year all its own, and he told me that if he ever sees his daughter again, he will tell her how sorry he is."

Miss Naseema had also mentioned that the general seemed weak and disinterested. "It's as if he has lost his will to live," she said, "and I believe it is because his soul aches for the daughter that he frightened away."

When Mr. Radhi visited me in October, he told me that rumors were circulating that I was hiding in Baghdad, and those rumors had reached British ears. "There is very tight security again, and those of us who know you are being closely watched, Ali. We won't be visiting as often because it isn't safe. I am sure they are following us, watching every movement we make. In fact, I took a huge risk just to come here and tell you this, but I don't think anyone was trailing me this time."

After that, the frequency of our old friends' visits did decline, and we were lucky to see one of them every couple of months.

⁎⁎⁎

March was the month when Mary was due to deliver our baby, and Kaka Hawazin had managed to forge some identification and documents so she could be admitted to a hospital. Neither Miss Naseema nor Madam Laila could come, which broke Mary's heart, but she understood and relied on Fatema and Sayran for support during the difficult delivery. My love was in labor for a few days and bled a lot, but in the end, she delivered a healthy little angel. We could think of no better name for our little angel than Laila.

It was clear from the first look at the baby that she'd inherited her mother's eyes and perfect cheekbones, and I thought she had to be the most adorable baby on Earth. I held her ever so gently, afraid that I might harm her if I even breathed too hard. Every glance at her made me love her and her mother more; they were practically identical.

As she grew, our angel was so sweet, a good baby who rarely cried and laughed all the time. Since I wasn't good at singing, I hummed to little Laila all the time, trying to teach her all the songs I knew, and she seemed to love them all. I enjoyed taking her out at night to watch the stars, and I whispered stories to her little ears about the beautiful house her mother and I had dreamt up in the velvet sky.

A few weeks after giving birth, Mary fell ill. The cesarean section had not healed properly, and it took her much longer time to recover than it did for most women. When she grew pale and weak and began to complain of abdominal pain, we took her to the doctor several times, but no one could figure out what was wrong with her. Not wanting to worry us, she tried to be brave and claimed she was feeling better, but I knew that wasn't true.

I had to do something to help my Mary, so I sent an urgent letter to Mr. Radhi. A few days later, and for the first time since we'd arrived at Kaka's house, since the day we'd escaped from Baghdad, Mr. Radhi, Madam Laila, Miss Naseema, Mr. Dalton, Mustafa, and my uncle were all together again, and Kaka Hawazin and his beautiful family were there this time as well. In spite of the circumstances, it was one of the happiest gatherings of my life, and I couldn't have asked more. They had all planned the visit carefully and would only stay one day. Kaka Hawazin made a feast that night, and it lasted to the wee hours of the next morning.

Mr. Radhi had read my letter carefully, and all of us men sat together to discuss the situation. I had told them that Mary was sick and needed better medical attention that she could get in our area. We all knew there were risks involved in taking her elsewhere, but her life was all that mattered to me. They all agreed, for they could easily see that Mary wasn't doing well and that something had to be done.

"I have to take Mary back to Baghdad," I said. "There must be some way to convince the general to help his daughter get the medical treatment she needs."

"I believe the general will help. He has a fine heart and has been remorseful for the harm he caused her and for breaking her heart," Mr. Radhi said. "Charles poisoned the man's mind and heart with his vindictive ways. I can approach the general for you, Ali, but you should not come back to Baghdad. Mary is the general's daughter, and no one would dare harm her, but there is great danger for you if you step foot in Baghdad."

"I cannot send Mary there without me," I argued.

"Ali," Mustafa chimed in, "you are my cousin and my best friend, but you are far too stubborn and hard-headed when it comes to Mary. This is not a matter to be taken lightly, because there is an official British warrant for your arrest, and you will be brought up on serious national and foreign charges if they catch you. What good will it do for her or your little daughter if you foolishly go there and get yourself arrested?"

"I can't leave Mary to face this alone," I said. "I have caused all these troubles for her, and I must accompany my wife in Baghdad."

We debated for more than an hour, and everyone had something to say, but in the end, we agreed that I would take Mary and my baby back to Baghdad after Mr. Radhi had a chance to talk to the general. Even if the general could not guarantee our safety or his assistance, I would take Mary to get the help she needed. I could not stand idly by and watch her illness worsen, and I refused to see her suffer any longer just because I needed to stay in hiding.

In the morning, we all enjoyed breakfast, purposely avoiding talk of our grim situation. Everyone laughed and ate, and as soon as we finished the relaxing meal, my friends from Baghdad got dressed and packed their bags to head home. Before they left, we all gathered outside, and a friend of Kaka's took a photograph of the whole group.

We all said our goodbyes, and Madam Laila hugged me tightly, as if she never wanted to let me go. I felt her tears on my cheek when she kissed me, and it was as if she knew something I didn't.

I pulled Mr. Radhi aside just before he got into the car and said, "No one has ever helped me as much as you have. Everything I have is because of you, and I respect no one on this Earth more. If you truly do think of me as your son, you will honor me by making Mary's safety your first priority. No matter what happens, I have enjoyed every minute I've had the opportunity to be with her, and I owe it all to you. Please promise me that if anything bad happens to me, you'll look after my Mary and little Laila."

"Of course, Ali. You are a son to me, and that makes them family. You have my solemn oath that no harm will come to them as long as I can do anything to stop it."

"I will always live in them, Mr. Radhi...always," I said before he nodded and got into the car.

⁑

Exactly five days later, Mustafa arrived with two letters: one for Mary, from the general, and the other for me, from Mr. Radhi.

The general's letter was short and only told Mary that he missed her and was eager to meet his granddaughter and that all would be fine.

Mr. Radhi's letter to me was a bit longer, assuring me that Mary would be taken care of because the general had promised to send her back to England the second day. He did mention that he wasn't sure what might happen to me. "The general says justice should be served, and that according to the law, you should willingly show up in court. Only then will he pardon you and withdraw the case," Mr. Radhi wrote. "He also requests that you do not mention that you are married to his daughter and that the two of you have a child, for he has already suffered enough humiliation and ridicule at the hands of his military counterparts over this matter."

At the bottom of Radhi's letter, there was a small note: "I promised you, Ali, the first time we met Mary, when you were already crazy about her, that I wouldn't interfere, and I haven't. Still, you know me well, so I am sure you will understand when I tell you that you should please consider…" And with the blank spaces, his letter ended.

I knew exactly what he'd intended to write. He wanted me to stay with Kaka, because he felt something was not right in Baghdad, but he respected me too much to interfere with my marriage.

Mustafa advised me that we would leave the following morning and would go straight to the general's house. In preparation for our departure, I spent the whole day thanking Kaka Hawazin and his family. "I won't be back," I told them. "No matter what happens, Baghdad has always been my home. Please keep my share of the livestock as a gift for little Sara, to help brighten her future."

A man of pride, Kaka didn't accept it at first, until I grabbed the ladder that night and asked him to climb to the rooftop with me. "See that livestock in the distance?" I asked.

"Yes."

"Imagine my family playing with yours on the other side. I've spent fifteen months with you, Kaka, and you have been my family. You have been an honest, caring friend and brought much joy to Mary and me, and that is worth more than all the cattle in the world. This is the least I can do to repay you for the stand and the risk you have taken for me."

We hugged tightly, and I bid that honorable man goodbye one last time and told him I hoped we'd meet again, in this life or another.

Mary and my child fell asleep around nine p.m., and I spent six hours writing this story. I feel compelled to say something here to the love of my life, and if things go awry in Baghdad, I hope these few words will bring her comfort:

Mary, my love, I will always be with you in the people who surround you. Take care of our angel, our Laila, and always look after yourself, my sweet, sweet rose...

⁘⁘⁘

Adnan turned the page but saw nothing on the next one, and he became furious. He banged his head on the table and screamed, "What? This can't be! Where is the end of Ali's story? What happened to him? What became of The Gardener of Baghdad?"

Desperate to discover Ali's fate, the book lover rushed to the back corner, where his old books were stored, and checked every volume to see if there were some loose pages there, but he found nothing.

He hurried back to his notebook and jotted down a few notes, then checked the names he'd already written to see if they might lend any clues. None of them were familiar or very helpful, and most of them were just first names of people who had lived decades before him.

With trembling hands, he looked at the last page again. Ali had stopped writing his tale on the morning of

July 13, 1958, the day before the revolution in Iraq, the day the royal family was brutally massacred.

Adnan checked his watch and saw that it was three a.m. He had to meet with his friend's old uncle later that afternoon, and he had so many unanswered questions for the man. He hoped the man would help, because if he could not, Adnan feared he might go mad. *I will get to the bottom of this, no matter what,* he thought. *No matter what it takes, I will find out what happened to Ali.*

With that obsessive thought in mind and a hundred unanswered questions swirling through his tired mind, Adnan drifted off to sleep in his chair.

# Chapter 6

Like every other day for the past several decades, Adnan turned the window sign to let everyone know his shop was open at exactly nine in the morning. He was still wearing the same clothes as the day before, as he had no time to go home and change in the morning and would have to wait till lunchtime to freshen up. He would spend an hour resting, shave his face, and he would meet with the old man at around four p.m. He hoped the fellow could help him solve the puzzle of the book that had left him thirsty for answers.

He had convinced his friend to bring his uncle to the shop rather than meeting him at the café. He wanted to talk to him in private and thought that a quiet place, with the smell of old books all around, might arouse the man's senses and draw out his most vivid memories.

Adnan closed the shop earlier that day and went back to his old computer. He was a lover of books that could be held in his hand, and he had never been much of a fan of the Internet. In fact, he found it difficult to cope with technology altogether, anything more modern than the television or the light bulb. He didn't even have an email address, and when he did have to type, he used only one finger. Thus, his limited knowledge of the World Wide Web made it impossible for him to search any of the names he'd read. Even if he had been able to Google it, he wouldn't have trusted the information; Adnan was a firm believer than any information so easily gained could just as easily be corrupted. He preferred to hear about old Iraq from the people who had been there and lived through that era themselves. Nevertheless, he spent a half-hour surfing through all the websites, hoping to learn some general information of that period in history, the days when Ali and his friends walked the streets of Baghdad.

Adnan stared at the monitor for a while, reading about the British influence in Iraq in the fifties. He read about Nuri Saeed, or Nuri Pasha, as they used to call him, the Iraqi prime minister with the iron fist. When the tiny print began to give him a headache, he closed his computer, locked his shop, and headed home.

The hot shower was quite a relief for the tension that had knotted up throughout Adnan's body, and it rejuvenated him a bit, much to his wife's relief; she'd been shocked to see him looking so fatigued after getting only a few hours of sleep in the shop for the past few days.

His wife prepared a large meal for him, more food than she usually cooked, because he looked like he could use the extra nourishment, even if it did put a few extra pounds around his middle. The delicious taste of her food and the love he felt from his family was refreshing.

Feeling better than he had for several days, Adnan kissed his wife and kids and headed back to the bookshop to wait for his special visitor. He was fully prepared to fish for the truth and was ready to turn over every stone in the country if that was what it would take to learn what happened to Ali and the rest.

A quarter past four, his friend and an older man finally showed up. "This is my uncle, Haji Abu Ahmad," his friend introduced. "Uncle, this is my friend Adnan, the man I told you about. He owns this shop."

Like every other man who had made the pilgrimage to Mecca, the old man carried "Haji" before his first name, very common in Iraq. The rest of his name indicated that he was the father of his eldest child: *Abu Ahmad* literally translated to "Ahmad's father."

Abu Ahmad looked his age. He was nearly eighty, a tall, thin man with a slight curve to his back. All his features were small, his eyes, nose, and chin, and his face was wrinkled. The front of his head was bald, but a few white hairs stuck out on the sides, and his thick eyebrows were as white as snow. He had no beard or mustache. He was dressed in a typical Faisaliya hat and a dark brown suit, quite a dapper ensemble for a man his age.

Adnan's friend excused himself and told Adnan, "I'll be back to pick up my uncle around five thirty. I hope that will give you two enough time to talk."

Adnan took the old man's jacket and helped him sit down. "Would you like something to drink?" he asked.

"A glass of water would be nice," Abu Ahmad said.

171

Adnan noticed the shiny white dentures Abu Ahmad was wearing; they gave him a nice smile. He'd been thinking for some time about the right way to approach the old man. He thought of Ali's story as an unfinished portrait, he knew what figures were drawn on it, but needed to know where to place them and what colors should be used to paint the backdrop. Bearing this in mind, Adnan started by asking the old man about Iraq in the 1950s.

Like his friend had promised, Abu Ahmad loved to talk. He was an excellent storyteller who remembered things in great detail, and for the first half-hour, he only stopped talking once or twice to take a sip of water. He told Adnan about the daily life of the Iraqis at that time in history, and more precisely, about the people who lived in Baghdad.

The old man's stories helped to paint a picture for Adnan about Iraq, a country that was just picking itself up from centuries of neglect during reign of the Ottoman Empire and the governments that followed. "Life was beautiful for some but not for others," the old man said. "Simple," was the word he used to describe that era. "Parts of Iraq were well ahead of many countries in the world, and some people were educated in Europe, but that was the minority. The majority lived a very different life." He talked about the lack of schools how difficult it was for people from various parts of Iraq to find proper education, compared to those who were lucky enough to be close to the rulers and authority figures at that time. "Most people at that time, especially those outside of

Baghdad, were people of simple means and led very rough lives."

Abu Ahmad had lived and grown up in Baghdad, so he talked much about it. He mentioned the places people went to: sports clubs, cafés, restaurants, nightclubs, cinemas, schools and universities, and markets. When he talked about the people, he said, "They were very passionate back then, eager to pursue whatever they loved and whatever lifestyle they wanted to. They didn't care about fame or fortune and only sought what would bring them pleasure in life."

Adnan didn't quite understand what the old man meant about the people being so passionate, so he asked him to explain.

Abu Ahmad gave plenty of examples. "Many musicians and artists flocked to Baghdad, the best of their time. Some were talented with their voices, others with instruments." He then talked about those who were passionate about athletics and sports. "There were weightlifters, wrestlers, Judo fighters, boxers, basketball players, and football players in almost every family." He concluded by mentioning painters and other art masters. "The people who lived in Baghdad in the 1950s were full of passion and ambition," he said, smiling as he remembered that time in his life.

Unbeknownst to the old man, Adnan compared every word Abu Ahmad said to what he knew from Ali's story. As he thought about those passionate people, he was reminded of Ali's love for his nursery and for the gardens in his city.

Abu Ahmad then touched on what was most important to Adnan, the great passion and love people had for their country and its Arabic identity. "The understanding that time was that, those who ruled Iraq during that time lacked that love of country," he said. "Yes, there were frustrations with the slow improvements the governments were making, but it was the Arabic identity that mattered most to the people here. In fact, I don't remember a month going by in the fifties when there wasn't a demonstration or protest, and they were all spontaneous. The youth and the older generation acted together, and the governments who ruled during the kingdom era neglected to pay any attention to what they were saying. That was the reason for their downfall."

Adnan furiously wrote notes as he listened to Abu Ahmad, all the while thinking of Ali, Mr. Radhi, and the general. As the talk went on, he began to connect the dots. When Adnan felt he had enough background from that period, he told Abu Ahmad, "I'm going to get a bit personal." He then went on to explain that he'd invited him there because he wanted to ask about certain individuals who lived in Baghdad at that time.

"Very well, young man," the old man said.

Adnan opened his notebook and read off some of the names, but none of them sparked Abu Ahmad's memory. "Miss Naseema, uh...Dr. Kamal—"

"Wait!" the old man said. "I know of a Dr. Kamal who held several senior roles within the Ministry of

Education during Abdul Karim Qassim's reign as president of Iraq, back in 1958 to 1963."

Smiling and glad they were finally making some progress, Adnan coaxed, "Can you tell me anything else about him?"

"Sure. Dr. Kamal fled Iraq in 1963, after the revolution that ousted Abdul Karim Qassim, and he lived in Moscow till he died in the early seventies."

"Excellent," Adnan said. "Thank you." He scribbled something down in his notebook then readied himself to ask the question he'd been aching to ask the first minute the man had set foot in his store. He got up and moved his chair closer to Abu Ahmad, leaned over and asked, "Have you ever heard of Ali, The Gardener of Baghdad?"

The old man grabbed his lower lip and began to toy with it. He thought for quite a while, and from his facial expression, Adnan sensed that he knew something. Unfortunately, the old man closed his eyes tightly, as if his memory was failing him and his mind was trying to travel back in the years.

Adnan was dying for an answer, but he sat quietly for a while and left his friend's old uncle to his thoughts. He decided it was best not to reveal what he already knew about Ali, at least not all at once, as he didn't want to influence the memories Abu Ahmad might recall and share. Adnan would tell him some of the details from the memoir when the time was right, but first, he wanted Abu Ahmad to remember as much as he could on his own. "Do you remember a problem during the late fifties, some trouble involving a British general's daughter?" he asked, giving him a hint.

The old man's face quickly lit up, and he smiled, revealing shiny dentures that stretched from one corner of his mouth to the other. "Ah yes! Ali, The Gardener of Baghdad. That's a name I haven't heard for decades," said Abu Ahmad. He asked Adnan to excuse his loss of memory, for the decades of wars and problems had taken their toll, and some of his recollections needed to be triggered. "I never met him personally," he said, "but I saw Ali several times in a café I used to frequent. As I remember it, he was a tall, fairly dark man. He had big, friendly, sleepy black eyes and a warm smile on his face most of the time. He was always clean shaven, and his hair was short, black, and straight, usually combed to one side. He was a man of strong personality, and he oozed confidence, but he was also quite sociable, a very generous man who was genuinely liked by several in Baghdad."

"Anything else?" Adnan asked, mesmerized as the fuzzy picture of Ali began to take shape in his head.

"He laughed a lot, and he made others laugh as well. Interestingly enough, he always dressed very elegantly for a gardener, and I never saw him without a rose in the pocket of his suit."

When Adnan heard that, he couldn't help but smile. He enjoyed hearing the old man's description, and he knew where it was heading, but he didn't say a word to dissuade him from talking.

"It was Ali who designed the Baghdad Pact square, the most beautiful patch of land in all of Baghdad. People used to sit there just to enjoy the colors of its flowers. As I heard from many, Ali was also a gardener for the royal family, and many said he was the best gardener and landscaper that Iraq had ever known." The old man stopped for a minute to take a sip of water, then continued, "That's all I personally know about him from seeing him at the café and talking to people who knew him directly, but there were many, many rumors."

"Do tell," Adnan said, his curiosity piqued.

"One day when I woke up, I saw British military everywhere, and word was going around was that they were looking for Ali, the gardener. No one really knew what was going on, as different rumors were flying around every week, changing from day to day. Some said Ali had married a British woman, the daughter of a high-ranking general. Others claimed he'd been caught and executed already. Still others said he managed to escape with the lady to Turkey. He was also accused of being a communist, and many believed he died in the 1960s, after the fall of that party. All I can say for sure is that I never saw him in the café again after the late fifties. I'm not sure when the last time was for sure, but I never saw him in Baghdad again after that. I think someone said he originally came from Diyala"

"That's correct," Adnan said. "He'd grown up on a farm there. Do you remember anything else about him?"

"Only that everyone said he made a huge impact on Baghdad," Abu Ahmad said.

Adnan was a bit disappointed. His quest had led him to a dead end, and the old man only knew things about Ali that he'd already discovered in the mysterious memoirs. In fact, the conversation left him with more questions than answers. With all the talk about a possible execution and Turkey, Adnan was completely lost.

There were thousands of thousands of people named Ali in Diyala, not to mention in all of Iraq, and he doubted there were any official records of the man that had survived the decades. In just the past four years, many governmental offices in Diyala had been burned to ashes. As the impossibility of discovering Ali's fate began to sink in, Adnan became very angry, feeling as if he'd wasted his time and someone had left the book there to torture him.

Abu Ahmad sensed the confusion and anger in Adnan's face. "Bring me a glass of tea," he said, "and I will think some more."

Hoping it might help, Adnan left the room for a moment, then returned with a glass of tea.

The old man drank the beverage and was quiet for ten minutes as he walked around the bookstore, scratching his head all the while.

Meanwhile, Adnan was busy writing everything the old man had said, cursing his luck.

"Write this down!" the old man suddenly shouted from the back of the store. He returned to where Adnan was sitting, breathing heavily from having walked so fast. "I remember that his full name was Ali Muhammad, and his uncle was Ismael Al Faris," he declared with a victorious look on his face, as if he was glad to realize he was still good at remembering names. "I remember it now, plain as day," he continued. "I was sitting next to them one day, when a younger person named Mustafa—Ali's cousin, I believe—introduced one of his trading partners, Abu Bara'a, to Ali and his father. I believe the trader was going to take Ali to India for some business. I remember those names because I overheard them." He stopped and scratched his chin again. "Yes, I am sure of it now, though I'm not sure if the uncle was from his mother's or his father's side."

Adnan replied, "His father's. Ali's mother never had a brother. Haji Abu Ahmad, thank you! Ali Muhammad Al Faris and Mustafa Ismael Al Faris. I'm sure this will help me find them."

Abu Ahmad continued, "I believe I can help you more. When my nephew comes, I will ask him to call my old friend's son in Diyala. I am sure he knows something about them."

Adnan's face lit up as if he'd come back to life. He kissed the old man's forehead twice and thanked him again for his great memory. He quickly went back to his office, called his friend, and asked him if he could come back at seven. "I need more time with Abu Ahmad," he said. "He's helping me so much."

Adnan kept his bookstore closed as he showed the old man the pendant and the book he had found. He then told him about what he'd read in the memoir. He felt it was only fair to share that with the man who had helped him get one step closer to solving the puzzle of Ali's fate.

Abu Ahmad called his friend's son later and told him that Adnan, a close friend of the family, would pay him a visit in two days because he needed help in an important matter.

Out of curiosity, Adnan asked the old man as he was making his way out of the bookstore, "Where were you on July 14, 1958, the day the royal family was massacred?"

The old man answered simply, "I was one of the many who stayed at home that day, listening to the news on the radio and the first declaration of the new government, hoping that only the good would come of all of that. Like so many others, I wished that the new era would be good for the people. Adnan...it has been fifty years, and I am still wishing for something good to come of it."

⁘⁘⁘

Adnan left Baghdad at seven in the morning to head to Diyala. He couldn't leave the day before, since his car plate number was an even one; according to the recent laws made by the new government to ease the traffic congestion in the city, odd and even plate numbers had to travel on different days of the week. It had been the longest thirty-six hours of his life, and he'd been restless all day and night. If it hadn't been for his lovely wife reminding him of the dangers of the public transportation in and out of Baghdad, he would have taken a bus, just to get there a day earlier.

He reached Diyala around eight forty-five a.m. On the way, he'd been stopped at six checkpoints. In the good old days, before the fall of Baghdad, it would have taken him no more than thirty-five minutes, but things had changed, and security was a necessity, since no one ever knew who was carrying explosives or when they might go off. As annoying and inconvenient as the delays were, they were for the benefit and protection of the people who lived there. Of course, some of the people who worked at the checkpoints abused their authority for their own gain or due to orders from the top, intentionally delaying traffic for one reason or another or treating commuters poorly, but in general, the checkpoints were not a problem for those who were doing nothing wrong.

Adnan met Haji Abu Ahmad's contact, and he invited Adnan to join him for tea at the café on one of the city's commercial streets. Most of the shops were closed, as Diyala was suffering just like the rest of Iraq. In fact, the place looked deserted, except for a few shops that sold necessities like vegetables and meat.

Adnan was very brief with the gentleman and quickly told him the names of the people he was looking for information about, Ali Muhammad Al Faris and Mustafa Ismael Al Faris.

"Al Faris is a familiar name," the man said. "I knew a person named Ali Mustafa Ismael, and he was from the Al Faris family. They had a big farm near the Diyala Bridge, near the river."

181

"Can you take me to that farm?" Adnan asked, quite sure that he'd found the right place.

The two of them arrived after a short drive. The farm had a big fenced wall, around ten feet, made of solid cement. There was also a black door made of steel, and it looked like a barricade; Adnan guessed it was meant to serve as a measure of protection.

Adnan rang the bell several times, but after a few minutes, he realized the bell probably didn't work. He shouted instead, hoping to get someone's attention.

A few minutes later, a young man ran up and opened the gate a bit. He stood behind it, looking out through the gap, and said, "Can I help you, sir?"

Adnan was sure there was some connection there, and he was eager to get inside those gates. "Is Mr. Mustafa here?" he asked. He wasn't even sure if the old man was still alive, but he had to try.

Much to Adnan's surprise, the young man answered, "Yes. Can I tell him who is here to see him?"

For a moment, Adnan was speechless. His heart began to beat very fast, and he couldn't even manage a reply. Overwhelmed with emotion, he took several deep breaths to calm himself down and said to the puzzled lad, "Tell him that I have come from Baghdad and that it is urgent that I meet with him—very, very urgent."

The young man then opened the door and invited Adnan in.

Adnan looked back at the man who had delivered him there and motioned to him that everything was all right and he could leave him there and pick him up later.

Then, Adnan made his way into the estate, hoping he would find his answers there.

The farm was beautiful and stretched as far as his eyes could see. After he walked 500 feet from the main gate, he saw a big, old house. The path from the gate to the house, the entrance was lined with citrus trees of all shapes and sizes. As his young guide led him closer to the house, near the garage area, he saw several large, sweet grapes growing on vines. The garage was covered with them, and the aroma was wonderful.

The two-story house was old but well maintained. The paint was nice and relatively fresh, and the windows were clean. It almost looked like two houses built into one, identical left and right houses connected in the middle. It was clear, however, that they had separate entrances. At first glance, Adnan guessed it must have had over a dozen rooms.

The young gentleman said to Adnan, "Rest here a while, and I will go look for my grandfather."

Adnan sat down on one of four beautifully carved wooden chairs, facing the west side of the house, where there was a blue and white tiled swimming pool. There was an ashtray on one of the smaller tables, next to a wooden chair that was different from the others, as it had additional pillows on the back and a footstool in front of it.

Adnan waited for ten minutes, and his adrenalin was gushing. He couldn't believe where he was. Finally, he heard some noises coming from the back, and an old man with a cane began to approach. Apart from his limp, the man looked well. His face seemed smooth, his hair was nicely combed, and he was well built for a man of his age. When he finally got to the table, he introduced himself as Mustafa.

Adnan couldn't control himself and immediately hugged the man.

Mustafa smiled. "You should never hug a man with a cane," Mustafa joked. "My third leg is only intended to hold the weight of one man, my friend."

They both laughed.

Adnan introduced himself as they both sat down.

"Please call me only Mustafa," the old man said. "Mister is a title for old men, and I wish to feel young as long as I can." He smiled. "Now that the introductions are out of the way, what can I do for you, Adnan? Why have you come all the way here from fair Baghdad?"

Adnan took the pendant out of his pocket and passed it to the man.

Mustafa looked at it for a second and opened it. When he saw the picture inside the locket, his face turned red. He used his cane to get back on his feet and moved closer to Adnan. "Where did you get this?" he demanded.

Adnan asked him to calm down and have a seat and promised to tell him everything. He then took the book out of his small suitcase. "Does this look familiar?" he asked.

Mustafa took out his reading glasses from his shirt pocket and placed them on his head. He took one brief look at the first page, then closed the book and said,

"My dear Ali." He then asked Adnan to come closer. After Adnan had slid his chair next to him, Mustafa asked, "Did you read this? Every word of it?"

Adnan nodded.

"Tell me about it, Adnan. Tell me everything you read."

Adnan began by telling Mustafa how he'd come across the book while he was clearing out his bookstore. He went on from there to share every bit of the story that he could remember.

Mustafa hung on every word, like a child hearing his first bedtime story.

"I can leave the memoir with you if you would like," Adnan offered. "You could read it for yourself, and then we could talk about it."

"I'm afraid my eyes have betrayed me, young friend. Even with the help of these spectacles, I can't read the newspaper headlines without getting a horrible headache. My ears work just fine, however, so I will just listen to what you have to say. You are clearly a lover of books, and I am sure that makes you a great storyteller."

For the next several hours, Adnan talked and talked. He remembered most of the details of what he'd read, for the story had been quite engaging in its own right, but whenever he felt as if he'd forgotten something, he looked at his notes or the memoir itself.

At times, Mustafa laughed, at other times he cursed, and sometimes his eyes glistened with tears. He was glued to every word, and by the time Adnan finished, he was visibly weeping. Rivers of tears ran down his cheeks, and he pulled out his handkerchief to wipe them away. Mustafa thanked Adnan for telling him everything, and then the old man got up and walked a few steps away, obviously wanting to be alone with his thoughts for a while.

After staring at the swimming pool for a few minutes, he turned back to Adnan. "Get ready for lunch, my friend, for you will need strength before you hear what I am about to tell you. It is a story with many missing pieces, but I believe we can help each other put it all together."

Adnan didn't understand what the old man meant, but he nodded out of respect and agreed to join him for lunch. .

They had chicken with rice and some kebab. The food was delicious, and there was far too much for only the two of them, but Mustafa insisted that Adnan eat his fill. "Ali loved kebab more than anything," he said. "He had to eat it at least twice a week. We used to go to a small place on one of Baghdad's oldest streets, a long way from where we lived, just to enjoy the kebab of Haji Hamza."

After they finished lunch, Mustafa asked his family to bring them some tea and biscuits and informed them that they were not to be disturbed during their talk. As soon as the tea and biscuits were served and everyone else had gone, Mustafa began to talk.

He started by telling Adnan, "That house right there is the one Ali and I lived in while we were growing up. Our grandfather built it before World War I, while he was in the military, serving with the Ottoman army. They gave him this land. Of course, the house was different back then, for there have been several renovations, expansions, and a lot of maintenance done over the years, but it has always been a big house, one of the largest in Diyala. Our grandfather envisioned all of his children and future generations living in it so that we could take care of the precious land that had been left to him."

"What can you tell me about Ali?" Adnan asked, hoping he wasn't rushing things too much.

"Well, you already know a lot from his memoirs, but my cousin was a very enthusiastic person of endless ambitions. Above all, he was a very proud man, justifiably so, though he seldom took any credit for being so nice and generous. Ali really helped me out when I got fed up with traveling and wanted to settle down in Baghdad. He paid the rent so I could open my shop. He was also very good to his workers at the nursery. Even while it was closed down, when he was in Sulaymaniyah with Kaka Hawazin, he ordered that their salaries be paid."

"From what I've read and heard, he sounds like an amazing man."

"He was," Mustafa said, remembering his cousin fondly.

"What happened to your cousin, Mustafa? I have to know what became of The Gardener of Baghdad."

Mustafa took a deep breath and recalled that fateful day, July 13, 1958. "I still remember it like it was yesterday," he said. "I ought to, for I've dreamt of it hundreds of times over all these years. That day Ali and his sick wife and baby Laila reached the foreigners' compound at around two p.m. Security was stationed around the complex, as well as in front of the general's house, ready to take Ali in for questioning and to face the charges that had been issued against him. The general came to the door, dressed in his military uniform. He hugged Mary and kissed her and the baby, but he didn't say a word to Ali or me."

Mustafa remembered clearly that Mary had stood at the front of the house and spoken in a loud voice, so that all who were present could hear her, telling her father that he had to keep his promise about their safety and that things would be all right. "You said that Ali's questioning is merely routine," she reminded her father. "Do not fail me again, Father, for I will never forgive you if anything goes wrong and any harm comes to me, my husband, or our child."

Mustafa continued, "We followed the general and Mary inside, and three British soldiers accompanied us everywhere we went, allegedly just as a precaution. Miss Naseema was standing at the door, and she and Mary shared quite an emotional reunion before Naseema picked up baby Laila. The general said we would have lunch and talk for a while before Ali's interrogation."

"Can you remember what that lunch was like?" Adnan asked, curious about the details and fascinated by Mustafa's tale.

"It was the worst lunch I'd ever had. It was served in the main hall room. Charles was seated in one of the chairs when we got there, and he had a wicked smile on his face, glaring at each of us as we sat down. As we ate, the general explained that Ali would be taken first to speak with the Iraqi police, and then an official transfer request would be made to take him to talk with the British, as it was a British matter."

"How did everyone react to that?" Adnan asked.

"As you might imagine, it was a very tense situation for everyone there. The air felt cold and stagnant, and the food didn't seem to have any taste. It was as if Death himself was dining with us or roaming around and tapping us all on the shoulder. Dalton gave me a signal to follow him, so I went with him to another room, where he told me something even more ominous."

"I'm afraid to ask what that was," Adnan admitted.

"And with good reason, my friend, for Mr. Dalton said he'd heard Charles telling one of the British soldiers that he was going to ride with Ali to the police station and that it would all be over before the interrogation even began. Mr. Dalton feared for Ali's life, and he told me that I should insist on accompanying my cousin on the way."

"What did you do?"

"Well, I went back to my seat at the lunch table and whispered to Ali to let him know what evil Charles was plotting. Ali told me not to worry and said he did not need me to go with him, but I refused to let him go alone. After lunch, the soldiers came to take Ali, and he asked for some privacy to tell Mary goodbye. The general told the soldiers to wait, and Ali and Mary went into the next room. The door was kept open, and everyone could see the love those two shared when they hugged and kissed. Mary was crying her eyes out, but Ali tried to smile and tell her everything was going to be okay. He kissed Mary's tears away, then asked to see his child. Miss Naseema took baby Laila into the room, and Ali kissed the child's hands, then said goodbye to his wife and daughter. He was just about to take something out of his pockets when the guards pulled him away. Somehow, Mary managed to get close enough to him to give him her locket."

Adnan was curious and confused. "What did Ali have in his pocket?" he asked.

"You don't know, Adnan?"

"No."

"It all adds up now, he intended to give her that treasure you found, that book you've been reading for days. That day was so shockingly difficult that for all these years, I'd forgotten that moment. Now that you've brought that notebook to me, I guess that Ali was trying to give it to his Mary."

Adnan was overwhelmed as he realized how significant the pendant and memoir really were. He had no idea what to say, so he remained silent.

Mustafa continued, "There were two cars outside. Ali got in the one in front, and the car in back was intended to serve as a backup, in case there were any problems or Ali tried to escape. When I saw Charles getting in the front seat of the first car, I insisted that I be allowed to go with my cousin. The guards refused at first and held me back, but Charles assured them there would be no harm in it, since it was only a thirty-minute drive and that he and the officer could keep us under control. I got in the back with Ali. There were four soldiers in the accompanying car, all of them armed, and the older one who was in charge sat in the front passenger seat.

"Nothing happened for the first fifteen minutes. I remember that well," Mustafa said, "but as soon as we reached the crowded city center, Charles whispered something to the driver, and he sped the car up, obviously trying to lose the car behind us. We knew then that something was wrong. Suddenly, Charles whipped out his gun and said, 'You humiliated me when you kicked me out of that party and stole Mary away from me, and now it is time to pay you back!' He told the driver to take a sharp left, onto a busy street, and to make sure to lose the backup car. Ali and I just looked at each other, then turned to look out the back window, only to realize that the car that had been following us was far behind, with several cars in front of it already.

"Charles bragged that his plan was working out beautifully. He also admitted that he was going to say that we tried to take his gun so we could escape, and he planned to claim self-defense. He took another look at the back and was sure we were not followed anymore, then shot one bullet into the air. He was about to shoot the second one right at me, but Ali pushed him aside. As they struggled, Ali was struck in the arm by a bullet, and the gun fell to the floor. The driver was about to hand his gun to Charles when I hit him in the back as hard as I could, causing him to lose control of the vehicle. We hit a parked car beside the busy street, and for a moment, we were all stunned from the collision.

"A crowd began to gather, and another car slammed into us. The driver was motionless, and Charles was moaning, bleeding from a bad head injury. 'I will kill you,' he said. 'I swear!' He repeated that twice. Ali pulled me out of the car, and I saw blood all over his arm. I remember hearing the shouts of the four soldiers who were supposed to be behind us. They were about 200 feet away and catching up to us. I told Ali to run, and he grabbed my hand and told me to tell everyone he was sorry for causing the people he loved so much trouble. He told me everything was noted, and just as the soldiers drew closer, he took off running through the crowd.

"Two of the soldiers followed Ali, while the remaining two stayed with us. They were confused and shouting, asking why the driver had sped up. Charles could barely speak, but he managed to lie to them and tell them that Ali and I had taken his gun and tried to escape. I told them he was lying and that he tried to lose them on purpose so he could kill us, but the man in charge told his companion to arrest us both for further investigation. I was handcuffed, and they were just about to handcuff Charles when he hit the soldier hard and ran away. The older soldier wouldn't risk leaving the scene to run after him, and the remaining two soldiers had taken off after Ali. There was no one left to tend to the driver, who had lost consciousness. I never saw Ali again after that day," Mustafa said with tears in his eyes.

"Do you know what happened to him? Did he get caught?"

"We were told that after five minutes of running, Ali turned himself in to an Iraqi policeman. He was taken to the station, but within an hour, was transferred to Abu Gharib jail, because the Iraqi police refused to hold him there, since he was such a high-profile case. He was transferred to the jail in a hurry, even without proper transfer papers." Mustafa then took a deep breath and continued, "The next day, the revolution against the royal family started, and sporadic fights broke out between the revolting army and the royal guard. There wasn't much of a resistance, and the army managed to overthrow the government in the end, leaving Baghdad in chaos. In one of the few confrontations, some sporadic bullets hit a fuel tank on the east side of the Abu Gharib jail, engulfing it in flames. Twenty inmates were held there. Four came out unscathed, nine suffered from minor burns, and seven were burned beyond recognition. We later found out that Ali was in that section, as it was the place reserved for suspects and people awaiting trial. Most of the paperwork in that department was destroyed, so there were no remaining records of who was there. The man in charge of the section was injured as well, and he later died of a heart attack." Mustafa sighed heavily and finished, "Adnan, you asked me what became of my cousin, and I cannot honestly say. Ali was never found, and although most of us didn't believe he was one of the seven badly burned individuals, the fatalities from the fire, no one could prove otherwise."

"I'm not sure what to say," Adnan said, gazing down at the memoirs.

"Me neither, Adnan. Your question is the same as mine. What exactly happened to Ali? When you showed up with this pendant and book, I hoped they'd provide the answer, but they've only sparked more questions. For instance, if Ali died in the fire that day, how did his memoir end up in your bookstore? Who put it there? I can only guess that Ali placed it there himself, perhaps when he fled from the soldiers after the crash. Then again, he may have dropped it, and someone else found it and decided to put it with other old books. I really can't say one way or another."

Adnan was shocked and began to sniffle and sob. It was a heart-wrenching story, and he was embarrassed to cry in front of Mustafa. He asked if he could be excused so he could walk alone, as he was badly in need of a cigarette and a few moments to clear his head. He walked around and around, trying to grasp the whole situation. He felt sad for Ali and couldn't believe the cruelty and bad luck he'd suffered. He'd simply been in the wrong place at the wrong time, and being burned to death would have been a horrible way to die. He thought of all those around the gardener, and he wanted to know what had become of them. He finished his second cigarette and went back to Mustafa.

Mustafa felt the sadness and fury in Adnan's eyes, as it was the same as what he'd seen lingering in the eyes of everyone who had known Ali and had been left to wonder about his fate. There was something Adnan had to know, and Mustafa made sure to tell him. He stood up, put his hand on Adnan's shoulder, and promised, "Adnan, within an hour, your sadness will turn to pride, and you will know that Ali's life was not one lived in vain. Although what happened was very tragic, many beautiful and great things came of it. Maybe no one remembers Ali, The Gardener of Baghdad, but the results of the events that happened to him and the actions of those around him are known to many."

"What happened to Charles?" Adnan asked.

"Please sit down and relax. If you'll be patient, I'll tell you all I know." Once Adnan was calmed down and seated again, Mustafa continued where he'd left off. "If there was a hero in this story on the day of the revolution and the days that followed, it had to be Mr. Radhi. He had the will and the power of an army. Mr. Radhi and my father tried to visit Ali at Abu Gharib, as they wanted to make sure he'd received proper treatment for the gunshot wound on his arm. That was the same day he was caught and a day before the revolution. The man in charge refused to let them visit him and claimed he didn't have the authority to allow it and that they would have to wait for the supervisor. He assured them that the bullet had just grazed him and hadn't done any sever damage to the bone or arteries, and that the doctor had stitched it up. I was taken to a different jail, and my father and Mr. Radhi tried to visit me as well, but visiting hours were over by then. In the end, they decided to try again the next day. They had no idea that all hell was about to break loose in Baghdad.

"The first thing Mr. Radhi did when he heard about the breakout of the revolution early that next morning was to tell Madam Laila to prepare several abayas and schemags, black and white headdresses. He intended to go to the Thompsons', as he was sure there was going to be trouble at the foreigners' compound. He wanted to transport Mary and the rest of them to safety, and he hoped the disguises would help. He had promised Ali that he would protect Mary and little Laila, his wife's namesake, and he would not break his word. He told Madam Laila to pack up their important belongings and documents. He didn't feel Baghdad was safe any longer. He passed word to my father to find Ali and me." Mustafa spoke with his eyes closed, as he was remembering that day by details.

"Mr. Radhi drove through the traffic and crowds to reach the compound, which was protected by only a few guards. There was no way they could handle the mass of crowds headed their way. He quickly went to the general's house. Everyone there was frightened, but Mr. Radhi told them he'd come to take them to Al Habbaniya air base, and he told them they had to move quickly for their own safety. The general resisted at first and said he was sure they'd be safe as long as they stayed indoors. He was convinced the British army would eventually come for them, but Mr. Radhi assured him that there would not be enough protection to ensure the safety of the royal family. The king had been killed, the British had

196

lost control, and they could no longer protect anyone in Baghdad. When the general saw Miss Naseema and Dalton running around and preparing to leave, he feared being left alone, so he began to gather his things. Mr. Radhi gave them the headdresses to wear so the crowd wouldn't notice that they were foreigners. Mary was still ill and was very weak, so Miss Naseema helped her dress, and Mr. Dalton and Mr. Radhi carried her to the car. Two hours later, they were at the air base, ready to evacuate an hour later."

"What about you?" Adnan asked. "What happened in jail?"

"Actually, I wasn't in jail all that long and managed to escape easily because when the revolution began, the guards left their post, and we were freed by the people who came to the police station to check on their relatives. My father was one of them. He told me what Mr. Radhi was doing to help the Thompsons, and he said our job was to rescue Ali. Unfortunately, we couldn't get to the jail, because all the roads were closed, and people were pouring into the streets, some celebrating and some just watching. It took us ages to cross some streets, and word was that the streets leading to the prison were completely blocked, because there seemed to be something wrong at that area. We finally gave up and went back to Mr. Radhi's house, hoping Ali would escape on his own and would show up there. We waited with Madam Laila for a while, but there was no sign of Ali. Mr. Radhi showed up at three p.m. and informed us that the Thompsons were safe and would be heading back to the United Kingdom within the hour.

"When we told Mr. Radhi that we couldn't possibly get to the prison to save Ali, he calmly told us not to give up. He decided to go to Abu Gharib himself, one way or another, to see if Ali was still there. Madam Laila would stay home in case Ali showed up, and I was to wait near Mary's house, in case he went there looking for her. My father would stay near Ali's nursery, and we would all meet back at Mr. Radhi's house at eight p.m.

"I walked to the foreigners' compound, and it took me an hour to get there. Everything was in utter chaos, and the place was a disaster. People had smashed the gates, houses were being looted, and some homes and other buildings were burning. There must have been thousands of people there. Someone mentioned that a Frenchman inside one of the houses had been killed. At that point, I thanked God that Mr. Radhi had gotten the Thompsons out and saved their lives. I waited there for a long time, but there was no sign of Ali, so I finally left around seven thirty,

"I arrived at Mr. Radhi's house a bit late, at twenty past eight. As I neared the house, I heard screaming and saw my father crying. Madam Laila was shouting, 'Ali, my love! My little Ali!' I ran inside and found Mr. Radhi trying to comfort Madam Laila and calm everybody down. I asked what had happened, and Mr. Radhi pulled me aside and told me about the stray bullets hitting the oil tanker and causing an explosion near Section A of the jail, where Ali was being held. He said that when he arrived, he saw seven bodies covered by blankets. The place was nothing but smoldering ashes, and the bodies of the deceased were unidentifiable.

At the jail, Mr. Radhi talked with the guard he'd met the day before. The guard told him there had been twenty prisoners at the last headcount, but the count from the previous day had been destroyed, along with several other records. He didn't know if any other suspects were brought in after the evening count, and his shift had ended at six p.m., so his supervisor had taken the late count. The supervisor had been rushed to the hospital to be treated for smoke inhalation. The guard then showed Mr. Radhi the list from the evening count, and Ali's name was on that list. He told Mr. Radhi that the fire had only been put out an hour ago, but in the end, it left seven dead and nine rushed to the hospital for injuries. The remaining four prisoners were thought to have suffered no injuries and fled. Some witnesses saw inmates escaping as one of the walls crashed down.

Mr. Radhi asked for the name of the hospital where the injured inmates had been taken, and he wrote down all the names of the prisoners from the last count. He visited the injured, but Ali wasn't among them. One of the injured men recognized Ali's name and told Mr. Radhi that Ali had been housed two cells down from him, but he didn't know what had happened to him or if he had survived."

"What about the supervisor? Did Mr. Radhi visit him at the hospital to see if he knew anything about Ali?"

"As I mentioned earlier, that poor man was of no help because he couldn't even help himself. He passed away at the hospital from heart failure, a side effect from all the smoke and fumes he'd inhaled during the fire. That left eleven, four escapees and seven dead. What we didn't know at the time was that Ali was one of them.

"The next day, we went to the morgue to see if we could identify Ali among the dead, but we couldn't say one way or another because they barely looked human anymore. We then searched all the hospitals and clinics in Baghdad, but we had no luck.

"We already knew who the nine injured were, so Mr. Radhi gave the remaining eleven inmates' names to the one of his friends, a policeman, and that man provided us with their addresses and the names of their relatives. We had to find out who escaped that day to narrow our search.

"We went door to door, as most of those on the list were in Baghdad. Only one was from outside Baghdad. After a week, we'd finally reached a conclusion. We were relatively certain that Ali was not one of the survivors of that fire.

"When we told Madam Laila, she refused to accept it and insisted that she knew in her heart that her Ali was still alive. She even put on her most beautiful red dress that day, a dress Ali loved. Till the day she died, she swore Ali was alive. Next, it fell to Mr. Radhi to do the hardest thing he had ever done."

"And what was that?"

"He had to travel to England to tell Mary. It had been two weeks since the day of the revolution, and she had to be told. Mr. Radhi told me that Mary was treated for ten days after she reached England and had finally healed from the infection from her caesarean section. She'd even moved out of her father's home with her daughter, Naseema, and Mr. Dalton. They'd all moved into her mother's home in London. Her mother was from a wealthy family and had left her some good fortune."

"How did poor Mary take the news?"

"The minute he told her the story, she did the same as his wife Laila had done the day they'd told her. She excused herself and went inside, changed into a nice red dress, and said she never wanted to hear about Ali's death again because she knew in her heart that he was alive. A few weeks later, all the seven burned inmates were buried together, and respect was paid to all, but both Mary & Laila refused to attend.

"A month after that, Mary called Mr. Radhi and told him she'd dreamt that Ali's nursery in Baghdad had been turned into a glorious playground for children. She wanted to use her mother's money, her inheritance, to turn the place into an orphanage that she would run herself. She was sure Ali would love that idea, as he loved helping people.

"Mr. Radhi told her it wasn't a good time for any British citizen to be in Iraq and that if she wanted to open an orphanage, she should do so in England. He said he and Laila would be glad to establish an orphanage in Baghdad and run it, as it was the least they could do in memory of Ali. Within eighteen months, both Red Flower Orphanages were open," Mustafa said with pride. He then looked at Adnan, who was a bit more relaxed. "Adnan, if it wasn't for Ali and his love story, those places would not be available to the children who rely on them. Ali's legacy has given a new chance at life to more than 395 children, and the number keeps growing every year."

Adnan smiled, realizing that Ali's life and likely death had not been in vain after all.

"Adnan, I know you're dying to hear the rest, so I won't keep you waiting. Let me tell you what happened to some of the people you read about. As you may recall, Charles escaped after the accident, but he was found on the day of the revolution, dead, with his clothes torn apart. It was said that he had somehow wandered around and had gotten drunk. He woke up in the morning with a hangover, unaware of what was going on with all the people in the streets. He had a fight with several youths, and before he took his gun out, he was beaten to death. It wasn't a good way to die, but he deserved it.

"Mary and her daughter are fine. In fact, I plan to visit them later," Mustafa said with a smile.

Adnan's eyes grew wide, and he started to say something, but Mustafa cut him off.

"Yes, they are alive and doing well. Miss Naseema and Mr. Dalton stayed with Mary and little Laila until they both died peacefully in their seventies. They were like family, loyal to the end.

"Kaka Hawazin and his wife died tragically in 1979 due to a road bomb that had been planted by one of the fighting Kurdish Militias. The tragedy of their loss sealed their daughter's commitment to carrying on her father's good name, and Sayran succeeded in doing so. She did well to take over their job and even expanded her father's work and opened a small dairy factory. She continued to stay in contact with Mary, and in the early 1990s, she opened an orphanage herself. Kurdistan Red Flower is now run by Sayran and Sara, helping more children in another part of the world.

"No matter how much good I say about Mr. Radhi and Madam Laila, it will never be enough. They were the most remarkable couple any of us had ever known, the purest, most caring, most generous people. After the orphanage was complete, they took very good care of the place and made it their life's work. They enjoyed every minute of it, and the children adored them. They had lost a son twice over in the death of their first little Ali and the Ali they knew later in life, but they gained over 100 children in return, and they served those children until the moment they died. They ran the place for over twenty-eight years, and they passed away eight days apart from one another, as if they couldn't bear to be apart. Madam Laila died in the garden of the orphanage while watering the plants. She was seventy-seven. Mr. Radhi died in his bed, holding a picture of his wife in his hand. That was in 1989.

"One of the orphans who'd been there from the start took over and did a great job with the place.

Unfortunately, the orphanage was closed after the fall of Baghdad in 2003, when it was looted. Luckily, the orphans were safe, with the help of Mary and her daughter, they are now housed at the orphanage in Kurdistan.

"Mary never married again, for she refuses to believe that Ali died in that fire. She used some of the money she inherited from her mother, as well as what her father left to her, to help children, and she organized charities and events as well. Her life was her daughter, her friends, and those orphans. She used to come to Iraq yearly to check on the place here. She always considered this her home, but she felt her mission was to help children in England while Mr. Radhi and Laila took care of the ones here.

"Laila looks like her in every way. She has the same lovely eyes, red cheeks, and hair. One look at her, and you can tell who her mother is. Laila studied Arabic and earned her degree in Arab literature. She speaks it better than you and I, so well, in fact, that she teaches Arabic at the university in England. She also helps her mother manage all the work. She was briefly married to a doctor, but it didn't work out.

"There, Adnan. Now you know all about the people you discovered in Ali's memoir, his book of precious memories. I must say that thinking back on these things, I have to agree with Mary and Madam Laila. Ali is very much alive. He is alive in the old walls of this house, where he once played as a boy. He is alive in the bright eyes of all the orphans who have been touched by the people he left behind. He is alive in the soil of Baghdad, soil that he once tilled with his hands and planted with colorful flowers. His body may have burned in that fire, but The Gardener of Baghdad is alive in those words that he penned, words that have been hidden for nearly fifty years but are found once again, thanks to you."

Mustafa then stood up, took a breath of fresh air, and fetched his jacket to retrieve a pen. "Please write down your phone number," he said to Adnan. After Adnan did so, Mustafa took it from him, grabbed the phone, and made a call. There was no answer for a while, but when someone finally answered, Mustafa said, "Mary, I have a nice surprise for you. I will be sending you a parcel by courier tomorrow. If you like it, please call this number." He looked over at Adnan as he gave Mary, Ali's beautiful bride, his phone number.

Adnan felt happy while listening to the conversation between Mustafa and Mary, not because he was proud of himself for finding the memoir, reading it, and taking the effort to find its rightful owners, but because he still couldn't grasp that he was listening to the heroes of that fairytale talking right there in front of him, major players in a drama that began some fifty years ago.

For the next hour, Mustafa told Adnan about his own life in the post-Ali years. "Of course I named my oldest son after Ali," he said. "After Ali's death, I came back here, back to our farm. Ali was right when he wrote that I hated working here during my younger years, but something changed later in my life. After my father passed away, I took over, and our business thrived for the decades to come. Now, I enjoy the peaceful quiet of this place, remembering the old days, and my children grow and manage everything. I am glad I was able to pass on generations of wisdom to them, and I hope they will do the same for their own children someday. That, my friend, is how people like Ali live on."

# Epilogue

Adnan had only met Haji Abu Ahmad a few days earlier, but the old man had quickly become a regular visitor. Every day around ten a.m., he dropped by the bookstore to have some tea and tell Adnan stories from his past. Adnan enjoyed listening to them, and he asked questions whenever he felt the need; Abu Ahmad was more than happy to answer whenever he could, and always in vivid detail that made Adnan's imagination dance in his head.

Haji Abu Ahmad was in the middle of explaining how hard it was for them to receive and send letters in the sixties and how happy he and his sisters were whenever the postman arrived in their neighborhood, when Adnan's mobile phone rang. Even though he didn't have caller ID, Adnan knew where the call was coming from.

As soon as he picked up the phone and greeted the caller, he heard a young woman introduce herself as Laila, Mary's daughter. "We are overjoyed and overwhelmed by the package Mustafa sent," she said.

"Words cannot express how wonderful it was to receive it, especially not over the phone." She told Adnan that they would visit Baghdad in a week, but they would only be able to stay for two days. Before Adnan could protest and warn them of the risky conditions in Baghdad, she replied stubbornly, "Sir, the decision has already been made. We are well aware of what our country is going through, but my mother and I both wish to pay you a visit. It is the least we can do, for what we've received is more than we ever could have wished for." Laila then informed Adnan that Mustafa would arrange a lunch gathering for them so they could all meet.

Adnan thanked her for her kind words and humbly said that he had done nothing that any honest man wouldn't do. He then asked about their reaction when they realized what Mustafa had sent.

"Well, I was sitting with my mother," she said, "talking about the orphanages, and the delivery arrived. Mom opened it and saw a book and a letter. She opened the letter first, and the pendant fell out. She was stunned and looked like she'd seen a ghost. It worried me for a moment, because I'd never seen her like that before, so I quickly looked at what she was holding. She read Mustafa's letter right away, just a few words explaining what the parcel contained. Then, she took me by the hand and led me into the living room like a little child. She scooted our chairs close together and told me we were going to ignore everything else in the world for the next few hours while we read every word in that book, written in my father's handwriting. Throughout the course of the next seven hours, we laughed, cried, hugged, and decided we simply had to visit you in Baghdad as soon as possible."

"Well, you are most welcome to," Adnan said, "even if it isn't the right time to visit Iraq. I only insist that we meet at my home for lunch. I would be honored, and it would mean so much to me and my family."

Laila agreed, and they both said their goodbyes.

Adnan turned to Haji Abu Ahmad and said, "Prepare your best suit, my friend. We have a date with history!"

※

Mustafa and Adnan were at Baghdad airport, waiting for Mary and Laila's plane to land at ten a.m. Mustafa had come to Baghdad the day before, along with his son Ali. They'd had a quick dinner that night with Adnan and had gone to bed early.

The next day, Adnan picked Mustafa up at exactly eight in the morning, and they ate breakfast together and rushed to the airport. Mustafa looked years younger than he actually was, dressed nicely in navy trousers and a white and dark blue striped shirt.

Adnan had been unable to sleep for the entire night because he was so anxious to meet the women, but he tried to look as if he was wide awake and only yawned once in a while. He hadn't thought of what he was going to say or what they would talk about. He was just looking forward to seeing them and enjoying the moment, and for the first time in weeks, his mind felt clear, albeit a little sleepy.

A late lunch would be held at Adnan's house at two p.m., giving Laila and Mary plenty of time to get checked in where Mustafa had made arrangements for them to stay. After they were settled, Adnan would take them to the bookshop to show them where he'd found the book, and he also wanted to introduce them to Abu Ahmad, the man who'd helped him connect the dots.

Just after ten thirty, two women came through the arrival gate. There wasn't a shadow of doubt as to who they were. Laila looked exactly like the photo in the locket, and both of them were dressed in red, Ali's favorite color. Adnan knew instantly who they were and called them over.

Mustafa hugged his old friends and formally introduced them to Adnan.

Mary took off her sunglasses, held both of Adnan's hand in her soft, warm ones, and stared straight into his eyes. She only said two words: "Thank you."

Adnan tried to speak, but he was too overwhelmed for any words to come out. The best he could do was look down and nod his head. Mary looked a decade younger than she actually was, and Adnan could see why Ali had written so many wonderful things about her eyes; they were unique, and never had he seen such green, shiny, sparkling eyes, like a doll's.

Mary and Laila said that they didn't want to waste any time and that they'd already rested on the plane and the bags could be kept in the car for the time being, so Adnan drove them directly to his shop.

Haji Abu Ahmad was there waiting for them, dressed in his finest suit.

Once all the introductions were made, they all sat down at the table where Adnan had first read the memoir that had, in essence, brought them all together. Tea was served, and then he showed them the back corner where the old books were kept.

They spent few minutes there, and Mary lingered behind a bit, for she felt her husband's presence there, as if he'd been there a half-century ago. She eventually returned to the others and sat down. She opened her handbag and took out a book and a golden-framed photo, the photograph of the whole group together at Kaka Hawazin's house. She held the photo out for Adnan.

He looked carefully at it, staring at each face and thankful that he could now put them to the names of the people he'd read about. There was Mr. Dalton, Miss Naseema, Kaka Hawazin, Fatema, Sayran, Sara, Mustafa's father, and the two he'd come to love the most from Ali's writings, Mr. Radhi and Madam Laila. Adnan's heart began to beat so fast that he thought it might beat right out of his chest. As if that was not already enough, Mary opened the book of roses, the flowers Ali had given to her all those years, and Adnan was once again overwhelmed by the love the woman still felt for Ali, even after all those years.

While the others were talking, shedding tears, and laughing as they spoke of the past, Mary took Adnan aside. "Adnan," she said, "you shouldn't sell your bookshop. Instead, go to Sulaymaniyah. Your family will be safe in Kurdistan, and you can stay there without any worries at all." She had already spoken with Sara, Kaka Hawazin's granddaughter, and Sara said she'd be more than happy to have them. "Besides," Mary said, "your wife can give Sara a hand with the orphanage. She can always use the help." Adnan began to object, but Mary said, "Do not make me climb a ladder and sit on a rooftop to tell you this." She paused and smiled, and he smiled right back at her, knowing exactly what she meant. "This gift you have given me of my husband's precious memories is priceless. It has reminded me of all the sacrifices the love of my life made to be with me. I have to make sure you and your family are all right, and it is only fair that you accept my offer, as I have more than enough to give. I will not allow you to sell your books, for your library is a treasure, and it will always be yours." She then explained to Adnan that his family could live with Sara for a while, until things calmed down in Baghdad. She assured him that his children's education would be taken care of, and if they needed anything, she was more than happy to provide it.

Adnan thanked her and told her it was a relief for him, because he loved his shop. "After I found the memoir," he said, "I took it as a sign that I shouldn't sell my father's legacy or abandon the place."

He closed the shop and locked it up, and all five of them left, heading to the hotel so the women could change and drop off their bags before having lunch at his house.

Everyone was quiet for most of the trip, until Mary said, "I want to reopen the orphanage here. I know situations are bad, but that is exactly when an orphanage is needed most."

"I know many good people who would love to help with it," Adnan said. "I will see what I can do."

They parked the car about a hundred feet away from the hotel, as Adnan couldn't find a closer parking spot. Adnan and Mustafa and the two women got out, and Mustafa spoke to Mary while Adnan and Laila opened the trunk to remove their bags. Haji Abu Ahmad stayed in the car, as he was too old to carry anything.

A group of old men was seated next to one of the houses adjacent to the hotel, playing dominoes. They stared at the women in red as they got out of the car and went to the direction of the hotel.

It was Abu Nasi's turn. His real name was unbeknownst to him, and his nickname, which meant "forgot," had been given to him by his friends in Basra, since he'd lost his memory as a result of an accident. He'd been told that he hit his head when he fell from a ladder, and since he had no recollection of his life before that day, his life started all over again.

At the time of the accident, Nasi lived in Basra in the middle of nowhere with his parents, who were in their early sixties. They had him very late in their marriage, so they considered him a miracle. After his parents passed away some twenty-five years ago, he moved to Baghdad and taught history in a school. He had

213

studied history late in his thirties, and his specialty was Assyrian history.

Abu Nasi was about to play when he saw that everyone was staring at the people who'd just gotten out of a car in front of the hotel. He turned his head and looked at the older woman in red and the old man who was talking to her. The old lady turned for a second, and when he looked into her eyes, something struck him. Confused, he looked back at her, and the second he closed his eyes, a vision came to him, like a flash from the past. In his mind's eye, he saw a beautiful woman on the edge of a boat in the river, with the sun shining behind her. He opened his eyes again, looked at the strangers, and his head began to hurt. He put his hand on it and closed his eyes again, hoping the pain would go away, but instead he saw another flash: two young boys running and running until they reached a small hut, which they climbed into and watched the sunflowers opening to greet the morning sunrise. He then saw another flash of a younger image of himself sitting on a seat with two slightly older people he couldn't recall, a man and a woman in their forties, holding hands and enjoying the view of a beautiful garden. The pictures began to flash very quickly through his head, and he saw himself again, standing in another place with the beautiful woman from the boat, giving her a red rose. Then he saw that same woman holding a newborn baby, a lovely girl who had the same green eyes as her mother.

Nasi's head began to spin, and he felt his heart pounding in his skull. He wanted to shout, but he couldn't, so he just held his head tighter and tighter and kept his eyes closed. Abu Nasi then saw another vision of his younger self, running through a crowded place, with his arm bleeding profusely. He was pushing people aside and running frantically, as if he was being chased. He ran into a small bookshop, went to the far back corner, grabbed a small book from one of the shelves, tore the pages out, and placed some pages from his pocket inside the cover. Then he put a pendant in the cover and carefully placed the book back on the shelf. He left the shop when a man began to shout at him.

Vision after vision rolled through his mind, all happening so fast. He saw himself lying on the ground in a strange place, beneath a blazing inferno and a shower of broken glass. There was smoke everywhere, and people were shouting. Some had already died, and their bodies were near him. An older woman who seemed vaguely familiar screamed, "My son is dead! My son is dead!" An older man tried to comfort her as she cried next to one of the corpses. The woman told her husband, "This boy next to our son is alive. He's bleeding, but we can save him." In another flash, things became clearer. That old couple became his parents that day. They took him to Basra and told him he was their own, reminding him often of an accident that had caused him to lose his memory.

Nasi suddenly realized they were not really his parents at all. He recalled having a different life before that day, before the accident. It was not completely evident what he was seeing, though, because it all happened too fast.

He tried to calm himself down and took a few short breaths. Slowly opening his eyes again, he saw the old woman several feet away. She looked at him as she turned around to make her way into the hotel, and he saw her green eyes clearly; in that moment, he knew he had seen her before. Another vision occurred to him, a picture of himself hugging a blonde lady with those same eyes and both of them crying as she handed him a pendant and said, "I love you, Ali." The name Ali kept on ringing in his head.

He opened his eyes again just as the women stepped inside the hotel.

"Come on, Abu Nasi. It's your turn...or have you forgotten that too?" his friend teased.

Ali stood and with a smile on his face declared, "Excuse me, friends, but I have to find a red rose quickly. I have a feeling someone has been waiting for it for a long, long time," he said before he walked away.

*"There is always love, no matter where we live. It is for us to find it."*
Ahmad Ardalan

I would like to thank anyone who had the chance to read my novel, and I hope that this story was the read, they had wished for.

I was asked several times, what inspired me to write The Gardener of Baghdad. I answered simply and honestly..

*"I was forced to leave Baghdad during the war due to security reasons known to all. After eleven years, I made my first visit back to Baghdad on business. The damage, and change in Baghdad was painful. My emotional response was to give back to my beloved hometown by writing a novel about hope and love even in the darkest of times."*

*A final note to all my fellow Iraqis*

"A nation that has a rich past, will always have a future. We are the oldest civilization in the world. We will rise again and live as one."

## About the Author

Ahmad Ardalan was born in Baghdad in 1979. At the age of two, he moved with his parents to Vienna, Austria, where he spent most of his childhood and underwent his primary studies. After his father's diplomatic mission finished at the end of 1989, he returned to Iraq, where he continued his studies and graduated from the University of Dentistry. As a result of the unstable political, military, social, and economic conditions in his home country, Ahmad decided to leave Iraq and move to the UAE. After facing difficulties to pursue his career in dentistry, he opted to pursue employment in the business world. Since then, Ardalan has held several senior roles within the pharmaceutical and FMCG industries, throughout much of the Middle East. His early childhood in a mixed cultural environment, as well as his world travels, increased his passion for learning about cultures of the world and inspired him to pen The Clout of Gen, his first novel. After eleven years of being away, Ahmad returned to Baghdad in January 2013 on a visit that was full of mixed emotions. Inspired by his trip to Iraq, he wrote his second novel, The Gardener of Baghdad. He did not stop there, as "Matt" his latest Short Story Thriller Series became available beginning 2015.

Other novels by Ahmad Ardalan:

Mystery Fiction **~The Clout of Gen~**

**"What if major events in modern history were planned decades ago?"**

Newspaper reporter John Teddy's miserable life is turned upside down when he uncovers a voice from the past—a voice that suspiciously knows far too much about the would-be future. John's natural curiosity to understand the hidden message takes him to places he never imagined seeing, and ongoing conspiracies he never thought existed. The more John gets involved, the more he is led towards mysteries that are beyond his understanding. The circle of people involved grows bigger stretching from west to east; each step forward is like a step backward.

http://www.amazon.com/dp/B008J0BSZO

Short Story Thriller Series:

**Matt Vol I:**

*"They murdered my wife two years ago...*
*Tonight, you die.*
*I am Matt, your nightmare!"*

On a quiet night like any other, Matt, a successful entrepreneur, returns home to his gorgeous villa, only to find his wife brutally murdered. A soft verdict against the culprits, a gang of violent teenagers, spins Matt's relatively calm and collected demeanor into something far more sinister. In a manic rage, he seeks vengeance for what has been stolen from him, and he lashes out against the weak system. Sleepless, lonely, tormented nights torture him, filling his head and his heart with frustration, hate, and anger, unleashing an entirely different side of the man--a monster even he did not know existed within him. From Berlin to Rome to Paris, the great cities of the world suffer in the wake of his wrath, as brutal, barbaric killings seem to be the only temporary antidote for his fuming, blood-boiling rage. His victims, so easily deprived of life, seem to be the only cure, the only way to soothe his yearning for revenge, or are they?

http://www.amazon.com/dp/B00QKVWNLW

**Matt Vol II: Chaos in Dubai**

*"They tried hard to stop me. But, even I can't stop myself"*

In the bustling city of Dubai, the new theater for his manic actions, Matt faces his worst enemy: a deep inner struggle for identity. Part of him craves the recognition a media frenzy and a new infamous nickname grant him, for he feels his murders are works of art that demand attention, but a love interest reawakens another part of him, reigniting an innocence he once carried within. Can love overcome hate in a city that prides itself on being a luxurious safe haven? As the end nears, which version of Matt will he be?

http://www.amazon.com/dp/B00RN69YX8

**Matt Vol III: Hunterman**

*"Am I being hunted?*
*Think again. I am Matt, I am the hunter.."*

The dark trilogy reaches its ultimatum, as Manic Matt approaches The Feds to takedown Hunterman.
Would they work with a serial killer for a better cause?
Could The Feds trust a man, half the world is chasing? A psychopath of many faces?
http://www.amazon.com/dp/B00V2GY40S

**Facebook Page:**
https://www.facebook.com/AhmadArdalan799

**To receive future updates on new releases and promotions, subscribe to my mail list:**
http://mad.ly/signups/130001/join

CPSIA information can be obtained
at www.ICGtesting.com
Printed in the USA
LVOW12s1606131217
559598LV00001B/125/P